THERE'S ALWAYS TOMORROW

THERE'S ALWAYS TOMORROW

ABNER NYAMENDE

PARTRIDGE
A Penguin Random House Company

To order additional copies of this book, contact
Toll Free 0800 990 914 (South Africa)
+44 20 3014 3997 (outside South Africa)
orders.africa@partridgepublishing.com

www.partridgepublishing.com/africa

CHAPTER 1

The evening was dark even though the weather was good, and the stars shone with all the brightness they could give. There was no moon, and the darkness played tricks with the two little boys crouching under a bush, which was standing at a distance of about 200 metres from the hut that was used as the kitchen and living room. The darkness played tricks with everybody who happened to be travelling on such evenings.

In the darkness, a stump of a tree would stand tall like a well-built killer. When a traveller bent down, the huge dark figure would also shorten, and when a traveller rose to full height, the dark figure would also do the same. When that happened, timid and inexperienced travellers would be so full of fear that they would break into a run, and as they ran, they would throw themselves into bushes and stumble over boulders, falling and bruising themselves, which would make them even more fearful, thinking that the 'killer' was at their heels.

The two little boys searched the darkness around them, and they listened to all those fearful night sounds that often come to life as soon as the darkness encroaches upon the land. Though darkness was part of their everyday lives, they could never get used to it entirely. It made their little nerves stand on edge just by being surrounded by darkness.

Now and then someone would come out of the hut to throw water or food remains into the dogs' basin, and the dogs would be heard crowding around their goddess, hoping to get something to eat. Then the figure would again disappear into the hut.

In the cattle kraal nearby, something coughed ominously—it was only a cow. Then they heard footsteps close by. At once they froze with fear and thought they were going to be discovered. A tall dark figure lurched past the bush only about a metre from the boys, then it stopped. Just when the boys thought they had been discovered and were about to scamper away, the figure moved on towards the hut. It was Speech, their eldest brother, who worked in Cape Town. He was returning from one of his daily hunting sprees for girls, together with the other young men of the village.

The boys were relieved, and for a brief moment, with their brother's presence, the darkness became less of a threat to them. But soon he disappeared into the hut, and again the boys were alone in the darkness. He had actually not even been aware of their presence out there.

That evening, not all the cattle had returned home, and so the boys had to suffer a beating from Gebashe's father. He had closed the door of the hut, fetched his sjambok, and went for the two boys Gebashe and Khaya. After raining blows on their buttocks, he had opened the door and shouted, 'Go find Zavela now!' The boys had scampered out of the door, howling with pain, and disappeared into the darkness. Now they crouched under the bush, and they were waiting for one of their sisters to come out and call them. That would be a sign that their sins had been forgiven for the day and they could come back to the hut for supper and sleep. They knew that the family in the hut was aware that they were out there waiting not far from the hut.

It took what looked like an eternity for Gebashe and Khaya to be called back to the living room. They sneaked in guiltily, following each other, Gebashe in front, and they sat cautiously by the fire.

'You two waste a lot of time playing, and you don't bring the cattle home on time. You see, now my cow has been left out in the open veld. Who knows if she hasn't calved by now? And the wolves will kill her calf, and we will have lost an ox!' said Gebashe's father as soon as they settled down. 'You must go and look for her immediately after school.'

Grateful that they had been forgiven for that day, Gebashe and Khaya replied, 'Ewe!' Then their eldest sister, Khubelo, gave them their supper, which they ate quietly and hungrily.

Such was the life of Gebashe as he grew up. He was the last born and was born when his father was already forty-four years old. When Gebashe was eleven years old, his father, Meshack, arranged for Khaya, his niece's son, who was then twelve years old, to come and live with them so that Gebashe would grow up knowing how to live and share with other people. So Khaya called Gebashe's father *tatomkhulu* (grandfather).

Meshack was a man of principle, and he brought up all his children with a heavy hand, making them earn their meals by working hard to produce mealies, pumpkins, and sorghum in the garden and in the fields. He was one of the early teachers produced by the Mvenyane Moravian Seminary School and Teachers' College, but he had stopped teaching quite early in his career due to a severe nervous breakdown. He received a pension of two pounds and ten shillings. He had built up his home himself and reared cattle, sheep, goats, and horses, which were the responsibility of the two boys Gebashe and Khaya. Now twelve years old, Gebashe was doing Standard 3, and thirteen-year-old Khaya was doing Standard 2.

For his mental breakdown, Meshack had gone to a medicine man, who gave him *isiqhumiso*—black powder mixed with animal fat, which was burnt in the fire and its smoke inhaled—and smeared the top of his head with a black substance. So his condition never really got better, and the family and villagers were used to him talking aloud to himself whether he was alone or in the company of his wife, children, and the villagers themselves. When he was sober, he worked hard to improve his home, so it was quite a big homestead neatly surrounded with palm trees, and there were fruit trees in the large garden. But when he was drunk, he was an animal, and he abused his docile wife and children most wickedly.

When he was sober, he was a blessing to his family, doing all the good things a husband and father was expected to do at home. But when he was drunk, he was the devil himself. Gebashe and Khaya feared him immensely, sober or drunk. Talking to himself, he would speak about childhood incidents and the history of the Hlubi and the Nyaluza dynasty. Nyaluza was Gebashe's great-great-grandfather and founder of KwaKhesa Village. His offspring now used his first name as their surname. Meshack would talk about anything that came to his mind, and what a volume of folk narratives he had. Gebashe and Khaya would sit on the floor next to him by the fire and listen to all those interesting tales.

Meshack would be the only one seated on a chair in his house, and his chair was the only one in the room. No one dared to sit on that chair even if Meshack was not at home. The women and girls sat on goatskin and grass mats, and the boys sat on the ground. All seven girls, his wife, and the two boys would sit silently without a word except to speak to each other in whispers while all the time Meshack was doing all the talking, which was not directed even to his wife.

KwaKhesa was in the district of Matatiele. The village spread out on the slopes of the Mjomla Mountain, which was facing the mighty Drakensberg. In winter, it was bitterly cold, with frost as white as snow on the grass, and the water in the mountain streams froze into ice. In summer, it was hot, but the grass was green all over, and there was underground water everywhere. The summer rains were a great blessing, but the severe electric storms accompanied by destructive berg winds and furious thunder and lightning caused much destruction to the crops and living things alike. But throughout all these seasons, the land was always beautiful. It was a mountainous country with breathtaking views and towering heights.

KwaKhesa was nurtured by its own culture, undisturbed by the routines of town life, with the town itself, Matatiele, being a safe seventy kilometres away. The white authorities in town had left things as they were at KwaKhesa. There were no tap water, no electricity, and no sanitation. All those things belonged to town life. Life at KwaKhesa was typically rural and African; it was what one would expect in a typical African village. Because of the mountain, the nights in the shadows below were dark on moonless days, and again because of the mountain, mist and fog were quite common.

Grandmothers would sit by the fire with the children and tell stories while the darkness outside constituted the domain of mythical creatures, giants, and the talking dogs of the ancient tales. *Ingcuka* (mythical bear) seemed to lurk in the darkness, waiting for an opportunity to snatch away little children and take them to never-never land.

Gebashe did not have a grandmother; his grandmother died long before he was born. So he and Khaya listened to stories told by his siblings and cousins. Gebashe enjoyed listening to folktales and was fascinated by the beings of the night even though he found them scary, and he is often assaulted by his exaggerated imagination whenever he found himself surrounded by darkness.

Gebashe was the last born and was separated by ten years from the sister who came before him. Meshack and Sarah had four surviving children, two others having died from regular diseases. However, theirs was a compound family in which children from relatives far and near claimed full membership. There was nothing unusual about this, as most families in the community were extended families. Gebashe loved his eldest sister the most because she told the most exciting folktales. Khubelo was already a fully grown woman and could easily have been mother to Gebashe.

Gebashe had no recollection of Gelesho, his eldest sister, who died when he was still a baby. Gelesho had been a very intelligent child, passing Standard 6 with a distinction and obtaining a bursary to further her studies. Her young parents, Meshack and Sarah, were proud of her achievements at school.

'Gelesho must go to my alma mater, Mvenyane, and train to be a teacher,' Meshack said to his wife.

'But, *titshala*, you are a teacher, and I have been a teacher. Can't she try another profession—nursing perhaps?' retorted his wife.

'Nursing is an obscure profession, and one has to go to town to do it. Teaching is popular even here in the rural areas. It is a noble profession, and every bright pupil studies to be a teacher. Besides, a teacher doesn't need an introduction in our community. No, she must go to Mvenyane and be a teacher.'

'But Mvenyane is so far away for our little daughter. She has never been away from home ever since she was born,' protested Sarah rather pleadingly.

But when the time came, Gelesho went to Mvenyane as her father had planned for her. Mvenyane was a Moravian seminary school and a teacher-training college; it was founded and run by German missionaries, men and women with resilient personalities who had worked against all odds to 'civilize' black Africa. Their forerunner, Georg Schmidt, who started Genadendal among the Khoi in 1737, had started an endless chain of stories of hardships, wars, rivalry with black chiefs, deaths, murders, and many other atrocities which his successors endured. The German missionaries were truly resilient people, and they had a single-minded commitment to what they were doing in changing the wilderness into a small-scale town resembling a European village, with the exception that the civilians were all black.

So before young Gelesho, Mvenyane stood on its six pillars as a monument of missionary endeavour on the African wilderness. That day, she had travelled the longest distance she had ever travelled by bus. She had been woken up at dawn on a Thursday by her mother, who had all her clothes packed in a wooden box. For the first time in her life, a chicken had been slaughtered for her provision, and she would have it all to herself and not share it with her siblings and cousins as she normally did. The bus, driven by Mnwana, appeared from beyond the ridge, and the family had to rush to the bus stop. It was still dark, and the bus, which was the only vehicle to be seen in that region, still had its headlamps on.

If one missed the bus, one would give up going to town that day as there was no other mode of transport and the town of Matatiele was more than seventy kilometres away from KwaKhesa. Men going to the offices of the Employment Bureau would start their journey at the first cock's crow, arriving in Matatiele late at night. They would then spend the rest of the night on the outskirts of the town and then come to the bureau offices in the morning of the second day. By bus, it was a four-hour journey, and Gelesho and her father were in town by nine o'clock.

It was the first time for her to see a town. There were so many beautiful buildings, streets, cars, and people whose names she did not know. In her village, everybody knew everybody else, but here it was different. There were numerous people going about their business and not even greeting each other. That was how busy they were. Her father bought a loaf of bread and a pint of milk. As far as he was concerned, this was indeed a way of giving his daughter a treat. She was used to making and eating *umkhupha* (mealie bread), but the town's bread, which was made from wheat flour, was absolutely delicious. To eat the bread, she did not really need the milk, and this she shared with her father.

Then they took another bus for a further seventy kilometres to Mvenyane in the Maluti Mountains. On the bus, there were other newcomers also going to Mvenyane, and Gelesho's father knew some of the parents accompanying their kids—those who had been at Mvenyane with him in his time. To Gelesho, this was new and strange territory, with beautiful mountains beckoning to her and wanting her to join them.

Late in the afternoon and after another four hours of what could have been an exciting bus ride to Mvenyane had it not been for the long and tiring distance, they arrived at their destination and carried their suitcases to the hostel. The journey would have been enjoyable to Gelesho had it not been for the fear of asking her father if she might go and relieve herself. So she suppressed the call of nature throughout the four hours of their journey to Mvenyane, and this was absolute torture. It was only when she was safe with the other girls that she asked where she could relieve herself. Then she was shown to the toilet. Had it not been for her quick mind, she would have been at a loss of how to use the toilet. Later, when she was already familiar with her new environment, a prefect gave them a lesson on how to use the toilet—that you do not squat with your feet on the toilet seat but that you sit as on a chair.

At Mvenyane, Gelesho was to live with white people and learn the ways of white people. Before that, she had seen white people only when she went to the trading post, which was ten kilometres from her home. She used to accompany her mother to the trading post about once or twice a year.

So her father said his farewells and left her at Mvenyane. At first she felt very lonely and missed home a lot, but soon she got used to the new rhythm of a seminary school. When it came to school subjects, she was top of the class as always.

One afternoon, just after Meshack had returned from the school where he taught, which was at a village about twenty kilometres away from his home, a former fellow student of his and now a fellow teacher, arrived with two strangers on horseback. Meshack had just unsaddled his horse, put away the saddle and saddlebags, and was enjoying a dish of sour milk. Seated with him in the hut they used as a kitchen-cum-living room was Sarah, his wife, with a baby boy in her arms. The fellow teacher, Sonqishe by name, saluted from the doorway, and he and the two strangers then got off their horses. After harnessing their horses on the fence, they came indoors, shook hands, and sat down.

'We have brought you very sad news, Nozulu [Meshack's clan name],' said Sonqishe after the usual exchange of health compliments.

'Eh! What news could this be?' asked Meshack anxiously.

'Er . . . uh . . . er . . . It is very difficult to say this . . .' stumbled Sonqishe along, at a loss of what to say. 'Er . . . You see these men, Nozulu? They are teachers from Mvenyane—Mr Nkosi and Mr Mlindazwe.'

'What happened to my child? Tell me what happened to my child? Is she all right?' demanded Sarah suddenly. The men had almost forgotten her while talking to her husband. As she spoke, she stood up wildly and put the baby down.

'Stop it, *MaRadebe*! We haven't even heard what these men are here for! Just sit down and take your baby, or else I'll order you to leave the hut,' demanded Meshack.

But instead of sitting down as her husband commanded her, Sarah wrung her hands and put them on her head. 'O, Bawo! Yini ngomntwan' am!' she exclaimed. Oh, Father! Oh, what is this now about my baby! 'Please tell me what happened to her.'

'Has something happened to my daughter? Is she okay?' asked Meshack, ignoring Sarah and turning to the men with urgency in his voice, being influenced by his already wailing wife.

'Yes . . . it's her. Gelesho has left us . . .' said Sonqishe hesitantly.

'What do you mean she has left us, Nzothe [clan name]? Has she passed away . . . ?' asked Meshack, looking confused.

'She had gastritis. That's what took her life,' said Mlindazwe, one of the two strangers. At this, Nkosi put both his elbows on his knees and placed his face in both his hands instead of uttering a single word.

'O, umntwan' am! Bambulele, Nkosi yam! Bamgqibile abathakathi!' exclaimed Sarah. Oh, my child! They have bewitched her, my Lord! The witches have finished her!

She wailed sorrowfully, running outside, having forgotten all about the baby, who was now also crying. Sarah ran to the edge of the courtyard, by now wailing at the top of her voice. The first neighbour to hear her was Nofikile, her sister-in-law.

'What's all this, *Sisi*? What happened? Why are you crying?' asked Nofikile as she came running.

The men inside also abandoned everything and went after Sarah, pleading with her to calm down. Only Meshack remained seated, his head between his knees and not even aware of the crying baby across the room.

In that commotion, Sarah's voice could be heard above the other voices, wailing, 'Yho! Bambulel' umntwan' am! Yho! Bambulel' umntwan' am! Yho! Bambulel' umntwan' am!' Alas, they have bewitched my child!

It was in the evening of a Friday when the bus stopped near Meshack's home. Then the men and bus conductors climbed to the carrier at the top of the bus. They gently lowered the coffin, making sure it did not tilt precariously but remained horizontal to the ground until it touched down. There was going to be an all-night vigil in the house of Meshack and Sarah, in which people would preach and pray. This was the community's way of counselling the couple, making their hearts become at peace with what had happened.

But Gelesho's parents could not come to terms with their great loss—their firstborn and their pride, who had been so dear to them. Sarah sobbed all the way to the graveside, and her eyes were red with so much grief and crying. All the women, including Sarah, wore white dresses and covered their shoulders with white shawls, which was an undying Moravian Church tradition. Everybody was sad, very sad, at the loss of such a beautiful and bright little child in her first year at Mvenyane Seminary School.

Chapter 2

Meshack did not show much emotion during the funeral. He had been brought up to be a man, and a man endures even if it hurts. His wife, Sarah, was completely broken down. Yet on the days following the funeral, it was Sarah who showed any capacity for recovery. Meshack would leave home at dawn and come back at night, drunk as a sailor. This drinking habit was a new mode of behaviour, and Sarah was at a loss of how to counsel her husband. Meshack got worse and worse, and finally, he became aggressive. He would attack his wife and kids with a sjambok at the slightest provocation.

One evening, Meshack arrived home and found the children playing next to the fire.

'Hey, you two! What do you think you're doing? Can't you see the fire?'

'We're playing, Father,' said Khubelo timidly.

'Where did you get the guts to answer me, you silly little imp?'

Silence.

'I asked a question. Where did you get the guts to answer me?'

At this stage, Sarah interrupted the interrogation and pleaded, 'Titshala, you are scaring the children, please.'

'Oh! So I'm scaring the children now? You sit here all day and spoil my children!' After saying this, Meshack leapt like lightning for the sjambok. He rained blows on the two little girls, and when Sarah tried to intervene, the sjambok sank into her flesh. All were on their feet in a flash, and the wife and children were screaming and trying to reach the door in order to escape.

At school, Meshack was always moody, and he punished the children severely for minor offences. Then at night, he could not sleep. He would take his spears and throw a blanket over his shoulder like someone undertaking a long journey and then disappear into the night. After two or three days, he would reappear, still carrying the two spears and the blanket. He now developed the habit of talking to himself aloud and claimed he was practising divination.

It took months for Sarah to convince Meshack that he must see a doctor, and even then, all he could agree to do was see a traditional healer. The medicine man gave Meshack *isiqhumiso* to burn and inhale the smoke. He made small incisions on all the major joints of Meshack's body and applied intsizi, a black substance mixed with animal fat, which was meant to remove the sickness. Then he gave Meshack some stuff to take in his nose. This made him sneeze vigorously, which pleased everyone as they believed that the medicine was working.

Sarah consulted Masewu, the chief elder of the Nozulu clan.

'Titshala just can't sleep at night. He keeps wandering around at night, and I don't know where he goes. I'm worried about his health.'

'I see. Maybe he is bewitched by people who are jealous of his work. That's why he should have been strengthened by a medicine man before taking up his job as a teacher,' said Masewu thoughtfully.

'Please do something, *Bawo* [Father]. He does not go to school any more, and the school inspectors will soon find out.'

'Has he seen any medicine man at all?'

'Yes, he saw Phuphethakatha. But his medicine isn't helping. Instead, things are getting worse.'

Masewu held his forehead with both hands, his elbows resting on his knees, and thought for what seemed a very long moment. At last he sat upright and looked sternly at Sarah, who was seated on a mat on the opposite side of the fireplace, on the women and girls' side. Then he said, 'Do you know Ezingolweni in Natal?'

It was a futile question as Sarah had done all her education and training in the district of Matatiele. She had never been to Natal in her life, but she answered, 'Titshala has been to Maritzburg, where he worked at the wattle factory.'

'There is a medicine man I know at Ezingolweni whose medicine is very good. Perhaps Meshack and I should undertake a journey to Natal.'

'Isn't that too far to go? Can't you go to someone in this region?'

'This one is an expert in treating bewitched patients. Meshack is bewitched, and so he must see this man.'

'When can you go with him? How long would you stay in Natal?'

'We can go in two or three weeks' time. I would have to make arrangements for my personal affairs here at home before I leave, of course.'

'Perhaps it would be good if you left at the month's end when titshala has received his salary.'

'That's a good idea. Now, don't say anything to him. I will talk to him myself. The month's end is only two weeks away. So I must talk to him this weekend.'

That was how Meshack went to Ezingolweni by the sea and stayed in Hadebe's house for three months. The traditional healer was an ancient man indeed, and he had much patience with the teacher who always refused to take the medicine and wanted to go home. By the end of the third month, Meshack looked and felt much better. Masewu spoke to the medicine man about starting the journey back home. The old man nodded and pulled his bag of medicine close to him. His ancient hand dived into the bag and came out with an empty bottle. It dived again and this time came out with a parcel of crushed roots. More parcels of crushed roots of different kinds came out at each dive of the hand.

Then he took a pinch from each parcel and put it into the bottle. Finally, he added boiling water and said, 'Here I have prepared *imbiza* [a bottle of medicine] for your son. He must take a tablespoonful twice a day—in the morning and evening.'

'I hear you, Mthimkhulu [clan name]. Will the young man get something with which to wash as well?'

'Yes. You see this? *Yintelezi le*. This is medicine for washing. He must use it twice a week. I am also going to give you something that causes sneezing. Here, this will help him.'

So Meshack returned home at last, but he could not resume his teaching immediately. He had taken a sick leave, and the school inspector had suggested that he saw a doctor so that he could obtain a sick certificate. He had seen the doctor before he went to Ezingolweni, and the latter had given him six months' leave. On his return from Ezingolweni, he went back to the doctor who had diagnosed severe depression. Dr Bower now proposed a sickness pension, and all was arranged with the Department of Education.

So when Gebashe and Khaya grew up, Meshack was already living on sickness pension. To augment his meagre pension, he acquired large fields and grew corn, pumpkins, and beans. He had a large stock of cattle, which the boys looked after. It was Gebashe and Khaya's duty to ensure that the cows returned to the cattle kraal every evening because they provided milk. The oxen and other cattle were only brought back from the mountains—where they were left to graze—when they were going to plough or do some other work.

Meshack was a hard-working man, but his only weakness was alcohol. When he was drunk, he would abuse both his children and his wife. He became highly sensitive and irritable. The children were terrified of him, especially when he was drunk. He would speak to himself and recount incidents in which he had been involved during the day.

Once, Sarah, after receiving a severe beating from her husband, packed her clothes and started her journey to her original home. When she had travelled halfway, she stopped, sat down, and thought of her children, whom she had left behind. How would her children cope in her absence while living with the devil himself? Then she started to pray, and her tears came flooding down her cheeks. Had it not been for Manqina, Masewu's wife, who came from the same clan as her, she would perhaps have continued with her journey. Manqina found her still crying uncontrollably, tried to soothe her, and begged her to return to her husband.

'Nobody has said it's easy to be a married woman, my child. You must return to your house for the sake of your children. Just think how hard it will be for them to grow up without their mother.'

After these words, Sarah surrendered her emotions to the old woman, who did all she could to bring her back home. When she got home, she found Khubelo, now the eldest child, sitting in front of the hut they used as the kitchen; she had her face in her hands, crying. The younger girls were all huddled behind the door in the kitchen.

Chapter 3

Speech, the second living child, passed Standard 6 and went to live with a relative to do the junior certificate at Lehana Secondary School. In those days, one obtained a Standard 6 certificate and proceeded to do three years for the junior certificate. Normally, after the junior certificate, one either went to a teacher-training college or started looking for work. Very few children proceeded to matriculate or get a university degree. So it was with Speech as well that after JC, he started looking for work.

Speech was only a nickname given to him by his father. His real name was Themba. After the death of Gelesho, his parents were no longer keen to educate their children for fear that jealous people might bewitch them. With Khubelo, they had flatly refused to let her proceed to do JC after passing Standard 6. So she was now staying at home, doing domestic chores and waiting for a prospective husband to come and take her for his wife.

Speech got a job with the Cape Town City Council as a storeman working in the Gugulethu offices. He lived with a cousin at No. 20 NY 3A, Gugulethu. If one was black, one could not live in a white suburb. One could only find accommodation in a black township. Samuel, Speech's cousin, had deserted his home in the rural areas of the Eastern Cape and had come to live permanently in

Gugulethu, Cape Town. He had deserted his rural wife and married another one in Cape Town. All this had happened about fifteen years previously. At his original home, they had no contact details for him, and after five years of waiting in vain for him to return home, his wife, who had no children yet, was advised to go back to her original home and start a new life.

When Speech arrived and was employed by the CCC (Cape Town City Council) office, he discovered to his delight that his cousin Samuel also worked there. In his first letter home, he mentioned his discovery but warned that Samuel had made him promise that he would not tell the people at home. Samuel, who was called Uncle Sam by people in the township, was now a highly respected member of the community in Gugulethu and a leader of his own church. He welcomed Speech with both arms and invited him to live with his family. Normally, Speech would have lived at the hostel at Langa Township like all migrant workers from the Eastern Cape.

Uncle Sam's wife, MaNdlovu, was a diligent and hospitable woman, and she immediately made Speech feel at home. Speech was an initiated young man, which made him and Uncle Sam bond quite well in spite of the age gap. He soon moved with the rhythm of the township and started having friends and girlfriends. Within the year of his arrival in Cape Town, he was at home in No. 20 NY 3A, Gugulethu. As their children were still young, Speech's relatives treated him as if he was their firstborn. Soon he was trusted with responsibilities like paying the municipal bill for water and electricity. He helped MaNdlovu go and buy the month's groceries, took the children to the nearby stadium to watch soccer, and fetched a sheep's head for Uncle Sam every Saturday from the merchant neighbour.

Speech's contract allowed him three weeks' leave in June each year to go home to the rural areas. He would spend the first of those three weeks travelling by train from Cape Town to Matatiele via Bloemfontein. He would then spend one week at home with his family and, at the beginning of the third week, start the week-long journey back to Cape Town. But for him and his parents, Meshack and Sarah, the whole exercise was worth it. Meshack and Sarah lived too far from the white people to find any fault with them, and Speech, like all migrant workers, was quite happy with the way things were at his work. He had accepted the fact that the white employees of the CCC were treated differently from the black workers and enjoyed certain privileges as white people. As far as he was concerned, there was nothing wrong with that; things were as they should be.

Gebashe and the other children were always excited when Speech came home for his vacation. They knew that he would bring them all sorts of interesting things from the city, plus lots of fruit, bread made from wheat, and sweets. On his second visit, he brought them a cuckoo clock and taught them how to read the time and how to wind it.

Like his sister Gelesho before him, Gebashe was a brilliant learner at school and grasped new concepts easily. So it was not difficult for him to learn how to read the time, and soon he was teaching the others. Speech loved his little brother, Gebashe, most of all, and whenever he watched Uncle Sam's children growing up in a civilized city environment, he wished Gebashe could live in such an environment as well.

On his third visit home, Speech had a proposal for his father.

'Father, I have been talking to my cousin Samuel about the possibility of Gebashe coming to live with us in Cape Town next year when he will be starting the junior certificate.'

'No, my child, I cannot allow your little brother to leave us while he is so young.'

'But, Father, he will be fifteen next year, and education loves him. He is now finishing Standard 6 at the local school and will have to leave you next year anyway as there are no secondary schools in our neighbourhood. The nearest secondary school is Mount Hargreaves, and it is more than fifty kilometres away from here.'

'My son, your mother and I have not yet discussed what Gebashe should do next year. He is going up the levels too fast for his age. We cannot allow our child to go and live away from us at such a tender age.'

'But, Father, you know he loves school, and education loves him. Surely you cannot allow your own child to miss a good opportunity for education when he is doing so well!'

'Remember what happened to your sister Gelesho? I'm not going to allow my child at his age to go and live with a person who abandoned his home and now lives like a detribalized city dweller, eating fish and chips and Lord knows what else! Do you want him to teach my child to run away from home?'

'Father, Samuel has grown up to become a civilized man and is now with a happy family and children who go to school. In the city, children wear uniforms, unlike the children in our rural schools. In the city, they have everything, and they teach the children to be civilized individuals who drive cars and own proper houses when they grow up, not huts like these that belong to backward and illiterate people.'

'My child, let us stop discussing this issue now. I see that Samuel has influenced you with his wayward and antisocial methods. I don't want to discuss this any more.'

And that was how the conversation ended, with both father and son heated up and angry. Without another word, Speech rose from his seat near the fireplace and left the hut in a furious rush. As an initiated young man, Speech was the only other man—other than his father, who sat on the only chair in the hut—who was afforded the privilege of sitting on a bench in the family hut.

But Speech did not give up altogether after that conversation with his father. The following day, he now turned to his mother with his proposal.

'Speech, you heard what your father had to say about this!'

'Mother, you cannot imagine the pain I feel for my little brother whenever I am with Samuel's family, watching how well his children are brought up.'

'Your father is right, my child. Cape Town is too far. You say you travel for five full days from here to Cape Town?'

'Yes, Mother, but the distance does not harm anybody. Lots of children travel with their fathers and brothers to Cape Town. What is important here is the opportunity for Gebashe's education.'

'Your father and I have not completely recovered from the bitter experience of losing your elder sister Gelesho.'

'Mother, nothing will happen to Gebashe. I will be there in person to see to it that he is well cared for. Please talk to Father about this matter.'

'My child, you know your father. When he says no, he means no. You also know that, as a woman, I can do nothing to influence his decision.'

'But, Mother, you can just try. Father is being unreasonable, and you know it. Gebashe himself would learn a lot about how to become a man when he is exposed to a different environment.'

'I cannot promise anything, my child. Your father can be very stubborn, and he hates it when I try to persuade him to do something against his will.'

And there the conversation ended. At the end of that year, Gebashe passed Standard 6 with a first class. His parents again arranged with their relatives in Mount Fletcher so that he could do JC at Lehana Secondary School. The subject of Gebashe going to Cape Town was never raised again, and Speech seemed to have given up getting his younger brother to live with him in Cape Town.

CHAPTER 4

The road from the town of Mount Fletcher to Mr Mbusi's home at Tsekong seemed longer than it really was. At fifteen years of age, Gebashe was leaving his place of birth for the first time to come and live with strangers. The Mbusis, father and son, were running private hostels for boys, and Gebashe was going to join the other boys living in this hostel. The Mbusis belonged to the same clan as Gebashe's family, the Nozulu clan, and were therefore close relatives to Gebashe.

Gebashe carried a cardboard box, which contained two pots, a plate, and mug; these were required at the hostel, where he was going to cook for himself. Also in the box were his provisions—a whole chicken and home-made bread, which his mother had prepared for him. His sister Khubelo carried a wooden suitcase, which contained his clothes and school uniform. The uniform consisted of a black blazer, a white shirt, a khaki shirt, and two khaki pants. They had to walk the five kilometres to the hostel. In the little town of Mount Fletcher, only white people and a few black merchants lived. The black communities, the Batlokwa and the Hlubi tribes, lived in the surrounding rural villages as far as Pirinsu, Zingcuka, Gxaku, and Ngxaxha.

Travelling on foot from the town to the hostel would not have bothered Gebashe much as he was used to walking long distances in his home village; only his father used a horse. The real bother were the senior learners who were travelling with them to the hostel. They travelled in groups, and in Gebashe's group, there were about ten other newcomers and about six senior learners. The latter were busy bullying the newcomers, eating their provisions, and making them carry their suitcases.

They called the newcomers cows and made as if they were holding on to their tails. After a few hundred metres, they would call a stop to rest. Then they would shout 'Bok!' at each newcomer, and the newcomer was instructed to respond by saying 'Mhe-e!' imitating the cry of a goat. The seniors would gesture with their fingers, and the newcomers were instructed to cry, 'Mhe-e! Mhe-e! Mhe-e! Mhe-e! Mhe-e-e-e!'

Khubelo was instructed by the senior boys to go ahead and leave Gebashe with them. Gebashe was the youngest of all the newcomers in his group. So he was spared the task of carrying a suitcase for a senior boy and only carried his cardboard box. They were made to march in line, and at the head of the line was a senior boy who would lead the line out of the footpath, up the hill, and again down the hill. The other senior boys used bushes to beat up the 'cows' that were marching in line.

When at last they joined the straight road to the hostel, they walked in a straight line until they got inside the reception hall.

'Hey, *kwedini* [you boy]! You are going to stay with me in my room and fetch water for me from the well. Take your belongings, and come with me,' said a tall very dark senior boy who was about twenty years old, addressing Gebashe.

Khubelo had just dropped Gebashe's suitcase and blankets in the entrance hall and proceeded to the living quarters of the Mbusi family to announce their arrival. She was to spend the night with the Mbusi family and leave for home the following morning. Gebashe was left in the hall with the other newcomers and the senior boys. So Gebashe took his suitcase, blankets, and box and followed the senior boy to his room.

'Good, you can put your things there, *jongwana* [little boy]. There is our bucket. From now on, your duty is going to be fetching water from the well for us.'

In this room, there were two beds. Gebashe was going to sleep with Manzana, the senior boy who had picked him up at the reception hall, and the other bed was used by another senior boy. The other senior boy, who Gebashe soon learnt was called Sonwabile, was on the quiet side and did not participate in the general treatment of the newcomers. The boy who had called Gebashe to come and live with him, called Manzana, enjoyed treating newcomers very much.

In the evening of that very first day at the hostel, all the newcomers were taken out of the hostel to a nearby field. Here they were made to form a line in which the boy that stood behind would hold on to the shoulders of the boy in front. In that formation, the newcomers would then sing and march while the senior boys shouted at them and beat them with bushes.

The song they sang was:

Leader: Ayivu-um' inyhurhu! Ayivum' inyhu-urhu! [Let the newcomer sing!]
Chorus: Vuma, vuma, nyhurhu! [Sing, sing, newcomer!]

Leader: A-ayivum' inyhurhu!
Chorus: Vuma, vuma, nyhurhu!

For the whole evening, the newcomers were thus treated. When the senior boys were at last tired, they allowed the newcomers to go indoors to eat their provisions. When Gebashe got into the room in which he was to stay with Manzana and Sonwabile, he found it empty. He was greatly depressed. He had never been treated like this before in his life. It was the first time for him to be away from home, and the reception he was experiencing made him miss his mother so much. He sat on the bed and began to cry softly. The tears just flowed like a flooded river and blinded him.

'Why are you crying, jongwana? Please don't cry, jongwana *maan*! You're going to be fine. All this is going to pass, and you will soon feel at home—like us,' said Manzana, who had walked in just at that time, unnoticed by the little boy. Hearing Manzana calling him jongwana made his tears flood even more. He just could not control them, nor could he help the state in which he was. Manzana put his hand on his shoulder and again said with what he must have thought to be a fitting tenderness, 'Don't cry, maan, jongwana, maan! Please! Eat your provision now.'

Without a word, Gebashe obeyed and opened his box, and when he saw the chicken and bread his mother had lovingly prepared for him, he began to feel so lonely. Indeed, he believed that his family had abandoned him and left him in the dark, unsympathetic world, where, all by himself and alone, he had to fend for himself. His heart was filled with sorrow and loneliness. Not even Khaya, who had shared everything with him, was close to him now. Only this stranger who called him jongwana was the closest human being at the moment. The Mbusis did not even invite him to come and introduce himself to them. Khaya was doing Standard 6 that year and continued to enjoy the warmth of home. When Gebashe left home, his mother was speechless, and his father had mumbled something like, 'We are carving a bright future for you, my child.' What future would this be that started with such a dark night?

At the cock's crow, Gebashe was woken up by Manzana.

'You must go and fetch water for us so that we can wash and cook breakfast before going to school, jongwana. Come, I'll show you where the well is.'

When they got to the well, they found other boys already filling their buckets with water. They had to wait in the long queue for their turn. Manzana greeted some of the boys whom he knew and left Gebashe with an instruction, 'Hurry up!' When Gebashe finally arrived in their room with the water, he had to prepare for school and cook himself hard porridge for breakfast. That hard porridge and soup was the staple diet in the whole hostel.

This treatment of the newcomers continued on the school grounds on the first day of school, and the teachers did nothing to stop it. This bullying was accepted by the school authorities. For the whole of the first week, the teachers were busy registering the newcomers, and there was no teaching for that week. This gave the senior learners time to abuse the newcomers.

Once, a newcomer was instructed by a senior boy from Johannesburg to push a coin on the ground with his nose. While he was trying to do that, the senior boy stepped on the back of his head, causing him to hit the ground with his nose. The pain sent him backwards, and he fell on his back. The senior boys left him sprawled on the ground like that, blood flowing from his nose, and joined other boys. The newcomer remained there until the other newcomers helped him on his feet. His nose was bleeding badly.

Soon Gebashe got into the routine of fetching water for his seniors and himself and cooking his food, which was always jabula soup and pap for breakfast and supper. During the week, they had their lunch at school. They ate meat in their lunch only on Wednesdays. The curse of being a newcomer was soon forgotten, and Gebashe started having friends to play with. His greatest friend was Khalane from Pirinsu. Soon he settled down to his studies and was again the brightest learner in his class. His Standard 6 certificate arrived from his primary school principal. It was inscribed in red letters.

Staying with Manzana had its advantages. Manzana happened to be a bully and was feared by other boys. They tended to believe that Gebashe was staying with him because he was his relative, and they dared not touch his jongwana. Though Manzana bullied the other boys, he had a soft spot for his jongwana and treated him very well. The jongwana's childhood problems, however, soon came back. He wet the bed every night.

'Try not to wet the bed, maan, jongwana, maan. Please, jongwana! Just try,' said Manzana when they were alone. As always, Gebashe just looked down and did not answer back. But miraculously, that night became the last night he ever wet the bed.

The first break Gebashe had was during Easter. He took a 5 a.m. bus from Mount Fletcher to Matatiele, and halfway between the two towns, at Kinirha Drift, he dropped off to take a thirty-kilometre road home through the mountains on foot. The bus from Matatiele to his village was to reach the junction at Kinirha Drift after 1 p.m. He could not wait for that. He missed everybody at home so much, especially his mother. He had so many stories to tell his mother and Khaya about Lehana Secondary School. By lunch, he was passing his alma mater, Sidakeni Primary School, and was left with only five kilometres to get home.

CHAPTER 5

On his second year at Lehana Secondary School, just when they were settling down for the first term, Gebashe was summoned from his class and told that he had a visitor. Not knowing who this visitor might be, he came to the staff room. It was his brother, Speech. Though he could not openly show his excitement, he was absolutely delighted to see his brother. It was nearly two years since he had last seen him, and ever since he had joined the new school, he had never seen him.

He and Speech kept a respectful distance between them. Speech was more than ten years older than him, and they loved each other as brothers only from a distance, without much that was shared between them. Yes, they did love each other as siblings, but they did not have to demonstrate that love. Gebashe respected his brother as a family elder, and Speech used to send him to do odd jobs for him, like fetching his horse when he wanted to take a ride. Seeing his brother at Lehana was as unexpected as if his own father would suddenly appear in his class.

'Come with us to your hostel to pack your things. We have a long journey ahead of us. You are going to Cape Town now. I have spoken to your teachers and to the principal,' said Speech after the rather awkward greetings.

'What am I going to do in Cape Town?'

'You will attend school there. There are very good schools in Cape Town, you'll see.'

Gebashe said nothing. But deep down in his heart, he felt a touch of excitement at the prospect of attending a school in Cape Town. For him, going to his home town, Matatiele, was a treat enough. Now going to live in a city was something more than he could imagine. The only nagging problem was the prospect of having to be treated as a fresher at a new school once again. Another surprise was that Speech was driving a car—a Land Rover. And he was travelling together with their cousins from the larger Nyaluza family who also worked in Cape Town.

At about ten o'clock the following day, they were in view of the majestic mountain from the direction of Paarl. For Gebashe, this long journey was tiring but exciting all the way. As he watched the scenery through the window of the Land Rover, it was as if he was experiencing a movie of his total transformation.

From now on, things would never be the same for Gebashe. He would live in a black township, go through non-white doors and gates and swim in non-white beaches. He would experience close proximity with white men like never before in his life. His father's cattle, sheep, and goats were now a distant dream. It was as if he had taken a huge leap from one country to another—from Africa to Europe.

At eleven o'clock, they were knocking on the door of Uncle Sam's house, having delivered their cousins to the hostel at Langa. Gebashe was received by Uncle Sam and his family with great warmth and enthusiasm. He was going to continue with his studies for the junior certificate at Fezeka Secondary School.

How Speech finally brought Gebashe to Cape Town was another story. The issue of Gebashe's coming to Cape Town had been closed long before he was sent to Lehana by his father. It so happened that the principal of Fezeka Secondary School, Mr Nondwe, came to Speech's office at the municipal stores at Gugulethu bus terminus. He needed the services of a plumber to install a bath in his house. Municipal workers would earn extra money by doing such weekend jobs. So Speech took Mr Nondwe's address and promised to ask someone to come and help him. When the weekend came, he and Mdingi, one of the plumbers, went to install the bath.

While they were doing the job, being watched by Mr Nondwe, Speech ventured to ask, 'Are there still any vacancies for new learners at Fezeka, Mr Nondwe?'

'Though there are so many children in the township, I wouldn't say our classes are full at all. In fact, the numbers have dropped considerably in Form I this year.'

'If I were to bring a child to do Form II, would you still take him, Mr Nondwe?' pursued Speech.

'We have already started teaching, and it would depend entirely on the child's intellectual ability to catch up. Yes, we can still take a child, depending on the circumstances.'

'Mr Nondwe, I have a little brother who is very bright indeed. He is now doing Form II in Mount Fletcher. I would like him to come and study at your school.'

'If you say he is very bright, then he would be welcome to come and study at Fezeka. When can you bring him?'

'In two weeks' time if you permit me.'

That was how Gebashe's future was decided by his brother, Speech—at the spur of the moment and without any planning for it. Speech took special leave from work, mentioning the passing away of a close relative who did not exist. Then he asked three of his cousins to accompany him. His explanation to them was that he wanted to show his father his new car, which he had recently bought.

His original intention was to try and persuade his father to agree to Gebashe coming to Cape Town with him. But when he got home and was face to face with his father, he lost all the courage he had summoned when he left Cape Town. It was then that he decided to abduct Gebashe and take him to Cape Town. The only person to whom he imparted this dark secret was his mother, who he was sure would never meddle in matters between him and his father. So all he told his father was that he had come to show them his new car.

By black standards, the car was new—though it had passed through the hands of four owners before it was bought by Speech. It was the subject of great pride for a while for Speech because, even by city standards, there were only a few blacks who drove their own cars. In the rural areas, only shopkeepers owned bakkies, and no black person owned a private car. So Meshack was impressed by his son's possession though he did mention that cattle would have been preferable, especially because he was paying lobola in order to get himself a wife by December.

It was only after Gebashe did not write him any letters and when Gebashe did not reply to his letters when he himself wrote that Meshack began to sense that something was wrong. When he mentioned this to Sarah, she pretended to be surprised and worried but did not dare utter the truth. Meshack wrote a letter to Mr Mbusi, the owner of the private hostel for boys. The letter was written thus:

> Nomzamo Trading Store
> Private Bag 347
> Matatiele
> 25 May 1975
>
> Dear Mr Mbusi,
>
> We are doing well here at KwaKhesa. We hope that you and family are also doing well. I am writing this letter to inquire about my child, Gebashe. I have written to him twice, but he has not replied to my letters. Is everything fine with him? We are anxious to know about his progress as he is still too young to be away from home.
>
> Please let me know what is going on as soon as possible and urge Gebashe to reply to my letters.
>
> I remain yours sincerely,
> Meshack Nyaluza

After a couple of weeks, a prompt reply from Mr Mbusi arrived. It was written thus:

> PO Box 50
> Mount Fletcher
> 5 June 1975
>
> Dear Uncle Nyaluza,
>
> I was glad to receive your letter of 25 May. We are all well here. We hope that you too are well.
>
> Gebashe was taken by your elder son, Speech, to Cape Town. He said that it was your instruction that Gebashe be transferred to a school in Cape Town. He left us at the beginning of March. We were delighted to see Speech now a grown man and working for his family after so many years since he finished school with us.
>
> Coming back to Gebashe's departure, we hope that everything is fine with him in Cape Town. He has not contacted us ever since he left us. But we understand that he needs time to adjust to his new school.
>
> Best wishes,
> David Mbusi

That was how Meshack finally learnt what had happened. In his fury, he wrote Speech a letter in which he harshly reprimanded the latter for disobeying him and taking Gebashe to Cape Town against his instructions. For disobeying him, he did not want to see him again in his house as long as he lived. He could arrange his marriage in Cape Town, but he must never set foot in his house.

CHAPTER 6

Speech made up his mind that he would face his father in December, when he had fully calmed down. He decided not to reply to his father's letter in an attempt to allow him to cool down. As far as lobola for a wife was concerned, he had a good job and could give his future in-laws money instead of cattle. The herd of six cattle that his father had paid the previous year were a sufficient token of the new bond between his clan and that of his fiancée. If his father still refused to let them have a wedding feast, he would simply elope with his fiancée and get married in a government office.

Meanwhile, Gebashe settled down to his studies at Fezeka Secondary School. He soon caught up with his subjects, and before long, he was top of his class. The teachers loved him and involved him in many of the school activities, including sports. He participated in athletics and also played soccer.

Mr Noyanda, the soccer coach, was particularly fond of Gebashe. Mr Noyanda was also his class teacher. During breaks, he would invite Gebashe to come to his house, which was not far from the school. Then he would ask him to wash his car, water his vegetables, mow his lawn, and do other such menial domestic chores. Mr Noyanda lived with his wife and two kids, who were both attending a local primary school. Mr Noyanda and his family came from Mthatha in the Eastern Cape.

'I want you to beat these boys in class as well as in the soccer field. I want you to have no competition in the right-wing position,' Mr Noyanda would say when they were together.

Gebashe was greatly encouraged by the warmth he received from his teachers, especially from Mr Noyanda and his family.

It appeared that Lion (as Mr Noyanda was called by the teachers and learners) liked the idea of Speech bringing his younger brother to the great city to study because, when the third term started in July, he brought his own younger sister, Naomi, who was twelve years old, to do Form I at Fezeka Secondary School. At first Naomi found Gugulethu a difficult place to live in. The township was crowded with people coming from different backgrounds. It was not like Baziya, her home village, where everybody knew everybody else. Here one met strangers at every corner. When she left home, she had been warned by her father never to trust the people of the city. So she could not trust even Gebashe, who had the responsibility of showing her where the shops, the post office, and the municipal offices were.

Soon enough, Naomi got used to the ways of the township. She and Gebashe were always sent together to buy paraffin, wood, or some groceries and to fetch and deliver post at the local post office. At school, they were always seen together, with Gebashe helping Naomi with her school work. Indeed, Lion congratulated himself for bringing his little sister to Cape Town because she was now getting good education and was receiving much help from Gebashe in her studies.

One Saturday afternoon, Naomi and Gebashe were sent to deliver a letter to a relative of Lion's who lived at Langa Township. It was late in the afternoon, but Lion wanted the letter to get to his relative that very afternoon. He had visitors that afternoon and could not leave them with his wife. They were to take a taxi to Langa Terminus, from where they had been instructed to walk along Washington Road in the direction of the mountain. They would then turn left into Mendi and walk down that street until they reached Rhodes Street. At the New Flats on Rhodes Street, they would then ask for Ngobozi at Room 10.

They walked on as they had been instructed until they reached the corner of Mendi Street and Rhodes Street. Here they came across a group of skollies talking and smoking dagga at the street corner. Just as they went past, the group fell silent.

Then someone from the group whistled and shouted, 'Mojo!'

There was no response from Gebashe as he did not know what to say.

Then someone from the group said, 'Hey, you two *moegoes*! Come here!'

Gebashe and Naomi continued walking and did not look back. The next thing they heard were running footsteps behind them, and soon they were surrounded by the skollies, who blocked their way.

'Hey, you! Why are you so stubborn? Didn't you hear that we are talking to you?' said one of the leaders as he started to search them. 'Where is the money, you idiots?'

Gebashe had money for the taxi for both of them in his trouser pocket, and Naomi had the letter for Mr Ngobozi in her hand. Soon all Gebashe's money was in the leading skolly's hands. After satisfying himself that there was nothing more in Gebashe's pockets, the skolly then went to Naomi and took the letter, opening it carelessly with his knife. In the envelope were a letter and five twenty-rand notes. The skolly put the money in his pocket, tore the letter, and threw the pieces in the street.

'Please don't take the money. It belongs to our elders. We'll be punished if we do not deliver it,' said Gebashe in a trembling voice.

One of the skollies slapped him in the face and produced a knife, saying, 'You think we're playing games here, don't you? Where do you live, you country rustic? Don't you know this township belongs to us?' Then he said to the others, 'Fellows, here are moegoes for an evening ritual. Let's take them to court for a fair trial.'

'Please let us go, *bobhuti* [elder brothers]. We have been sent by the elders to take an important message to someone at New Flats,' said Naomi, starting to cry softly.

'Hey, shut up, you *skhebereshe*,' said one of the skollies coldly.

Gebashe was himself gripped with fear. He did not know what to do. Now that all the money was gone and the purpose of their mission destroyed, all he was concerned with was that they both got out of the situation alive. He did not know what the skollies meant about a court trial. But he was sure they were planning some mischief for them. He had Naomi to protect and both their lives to save. The skollies started escorting them through the alleys of the township, moving towards the back streets. There were men standing in front of a block of flats, conversing and playing morabaraba. Gebashe hoped against hope that the men would see what was happening to them and come to their rescue. Some of the men just looked casually in their direction and went back to their game. One of the skollies had placed his arm around Gebashe's neck as if they were in conversation, and his right hand was holding a knife against Gebashe's ribs. Naomi too was escorted in the same way by another skollie.

About 500 metres from the back street of the township was the beginning of a jungle of wild trees and bushes. A narrow footpath led from the township to the jungle. This narrow footpath was used during the week by people who wanted to get firewood for their stoves in winter. On weekends, it was completely deserted; township people feared the jungle as it was the home for skollies. Every now and again, dead bodies of victims of the skollies were often discovered by the police. Still many people were known to have disappeared in the jungle without a trace.

Now when the skollies reached the back street, they escorted their two victims on the now deserted footpath to the jungle. There was no trace of life outside the houses in the township. It was a Sunday afternoon; people were indoors, and the township looked dead. Naomi looked back longingly at the smoke rising from the chimneys of the little township houses. There were life and security there. But if she screamed, nobody would come to their rescue. Everybody was terrified of the skollies. They ruled the townships with an iron fist—the iron being the knife blade in the fist of a skolly. A hand pushed Naomi roughly, and she was ordered not to look back; otherwise, her throat would be slit open.

The jungle was dead silent as if already in mourning for the crime that was to be committed. No birds sang, and the few birds that were in the middle of the jungle hid themselves behind the leaves and looked up into the sky. Gebashe sighed and despair gripped him tight. They reached an open space in the middle of the jungle, where the skollies formed a circle around Naomi and Gebashe. By way of starting their ritual, they passed *zolies* of dagga from one to the other, and every one of them took a pinch of heroin.

All this time, Naomi was crying and shivering, and Gebashe was pleading: 'O, yini! Can't you please just let us go? We'll say nothing about you at home!'

'Shut up, moegoe! You haven't seen anything yet!' said the leader, the one they called Ta Eja. 'You, skhebereshe! Take off your clothes!'

Naomi hesitated and looked at him pleadingly. Ta Eja slapped her hard in her face and put the point of his knife at her throat. 'Did you hear what I said? Take off your clothes—now!' said Ta Eja menacingly.

Naomi started to pull her dress off slowly and fearfully. When she had finished, she was left in her petticoat. Again Ta Eja slapped her hard on her jaw, and the heavy blow sent her reeling to the ground. 'I said take off your clothes!'

Naomi rose painfully to her feet. She felt a weakness in her knees. Her nose was bleeding from the first blow Ta Eja had given her between the eyes. She started to take off her petticoat and was now left with panties.

'Take off the panties!' said Ta Eja, grinning wickedly. Her breasts had begun to develop though they were not fully grown yet, and pubic hair at her groin was starting to show. 'Lie down! Not on your stomach—on your back, you bitch! Joe and Storie, keep an eye on the boy,' said Ta Eja, moving forward and undoing the belt on his trousers.

Gebashe had been thinking it was clear that they were going to kill them. There was nobody to save them in the jungle. Lion and his brother, Speech, would only be alerted when they did not return in the evening. He must do something to save their lives. There were seven of them altogether, and they were older than him. What could he do against these odds? Near the feet of one of them, there was a small dry branch that had fallen off a tree. Maybe he could use that as a stick. Gebashe had grown up in the rural areas, and he was good at stick fighting. Maybe this was his only chance.

He dived suddenly and unexpectedly, and before the skollies were aware what was happening, he had the branch in his firm grip. The first one to recover came to him with knife in hand, the left hand ready to block the branch. Gebashe saw that the skolly was only protecting his head, and he sent the branch flying to the rascal's knee, striking him a full blow. The rascal screamed and sagged to the ground, which gave Gebashe the opportunity he wanted, and he struck him squarely on the forehead, opening a wide gash. Blood gushed out immediately while Gebashe turned to the next one. He was almost too late to face the other fellow because the rascal was already too close to him to give him a chance to strike a blow with the stick. The rascal tried to grab both his arms, and he wrestled with him, but then another one came from behind and pinned his arms against his body, rendering him completely helpless. They tripped him, and as he fell, they all went for him.

Meanwhile Naomi rose to her feet and started to run. She then realized that she was stark naked, and after taking a few steps into the jungle, she dashed back, hoping to grab her dress from the ground. Ta Eja was already waiting for her, and he struck her with a fist this time, dropping her to the ground. Then he kicked her mercilessly in the face. Her screams were simply lost in the jungle. Ta Eja kicked her until her body was limp and she lost consciousness. Her face was now covered with blood.

Gebashe realized that he was not going to live for long in these circumstances. The most unsettling injury was a stab wound in his stomach. The gash was so wide that the intestines were just lolling out. There were other stab wounds in his body, but he did not know how serious they were. He lay there, feeling dizzy. And when he realized that the skollies were gang-raping Naomi, his body could not take it, and he sensed that he could barely focus. The last thing he heard was what sounded like a cracking noise, and he lost consciousness.

First, he sensed a strong light behind his eyelids and felt the need to open them. He tried to open his eyes but was assaulted by this blinding light. When he heard his name being called as if in a whisper, he forced himself to open his eyes. At first, he saw just a blur, but slowly a figure materialized before him. It was Speech leaning over the hospital bed. So he was back in the world of stories and was now listening to his own story being told to him by Speech and Lion.

They had been lost for three days, and Speech and Lion had launched a massive manhunt. On the third day, they found them at Groote Schuur Hospital, with stab wounds and other injuries. Naomi, who was now in the female ward, had been raped, but she had regained consciousness a day before Speech and Lion found them. Gebashe had been in a coma for five days. They had almost given up on him. On their part, Naomi and Gebashe could only tell the story to the time they lost consciousness. Whatever happened thereafter, nobody knew.

CHAPTER 7

Speech and Gebashe lived in a room built in the yard by their cousin Uncle Sam. As close relatives, they were not paying rent while the other people who occupied rooms in the yard paid rent to Uncle Sam. Gebashe would be sent to the shop to buy items like paraffin, salt, toilet paper, milk, etc. On Saturdays, he would help with the cleaning of his brother's car and Uncle Sam's car. Then he would be off to NY 75 to help Lion with his tasks. NY 75 was the street in which Fezeka was also situated. Gebashe and Naomi would do their homework while Lion listened to the radio in the lounge. He liked boxing matches, which were frequently broadcast on weekends. Mrs Noyanda was always busy in the kitchen while the kids would be playing in the yard.

'How much did you score in the maths test?' asked Naomi.

'Seventeen out of twenty. The test wasn't bad at all because it was based on what we did last week. I lost the three points due to careless mistakes. How much did you get in your biology test?'

'Fourteen out of twenty. I like biology, but I hate maths. I just cannot understand Mr Mosala. And what's even worse, they are far ahead here with the syllabus than at All Saints, where I was.'

'You've got to catch up, Naomi. Maths is very important if you want to get a good job.'

'Is all this pain in order to get a good job? I don't understand.'

'To have a good job, a house of your own, a car, a husband, and children. Don't you see how happy Lion is? He is enjoying a good life.'

'Why do you have to go to school to enjoy such a life? Do ordinary people who work in factories and construction companies miss anything in life? I mean, they too have money to buy cars and build homes, so they can live happily with their wives and children.'

'Life isn't rich enough when you are illiterate. There are many things that you do not understand. What do you want to be when you are grown up, Naomi?'

'I want to be a nurse and wear a white uniform. And you? What do you want to be?'

'I don't know. A teacher maybe. My father was a teacher, and everybody agrees it's a noble profession.'

'Oh, I don't like teaching. It's too much work, and the schoolkids can be so disobedient,' said Naomi as she looked at Gebashe with those beautiful smiling eyes. She had a brown complexion, and she could easily pass as a coloured person; her face promised unsurpassed beauty in the future when she would have her own money to look after herself. She had a calm beauty that commanded much respect and dignity even at her young age.

On Friday afternoons, the learners were allowed to play sports in the schoolyard as there was no teaching taking place. The whole yard would be full of learners doing different things. Normally, Gebashe would be playing soccer with his friends. It was on one of those Fridays that something happened which changed Gebashe's life for good.

The fence of the schoolyard ran along NY 75. Opening into NY 75 was the main gate of the school, which was used by pedestrians and motorists. In the west, NY 75 ran into NY 1, the main street of Gugulethu, and in the east, the street went into a T-junction with NY 72, which ran parallel to NY 1, linking Lansdowne Road to NY 3. On the western side of NY 1, where NY 75 formed a T-junction with NY 1, there were migrant workers' hostels.

Gebashe was busy manoeuvring the ball towards the goals when he suddenly realized that the goalkeeper was not watching the ball at all but was instead staring in the direction of the main gate. Then without again looking at the ball, he made a dash for the main gate. When Gebashe looked in the direction of the main gate, he saw a group of schoolboys gathered around someone in the street outside the schoolyard. Already the rest of the boys who had been playing soccer with him were running towards the growing crowd.

'Gebashe, come and see!' shouted Mandla, one of the boys that had been playing soccer with him. Mandla had already started running towards the main gate as he spoke. Being curious about what was happening, Gebashe abandoned the game and ran towards the crowd of boys outside the schoolyard.

When Gebashe got there, he found himself at the back of the crowd and could only see the upper body of a man who was wearing a municipal worker's overall. He could not make out what it was he was concentrating on. It appeared that the man was just finishing whatever he was doing because he now straightened up, and one of the boys near him started to chant, accompanying this with hand-clapping. The boys surrounding the man took up the chanting and hand-clapping, and the man started to march and dance.

Leader: Hee-e, Sphithi!
Chorus: Sphithi, kwenze njani?
Leader: Hee-e, Sphithi!
Chorus: Hee-e, Sphithi, kwenze njani?
Dancer: Hu! Hu! Hu! Hu!

Then the man marched along the street in the direction of NY 1, with the crowd of boys chanting and clapping hands. Still puzzled by what was taking place, Gebashe moved along with the chanting crowd. He found himself close to Mandla, who was chanting and clapping enthusiastically.

'Mandla, what is going on? Is this a madman?' asked Gebashe, tugging at Mandla's jacket to try and draw his attention.

'Yes, he's crazy. He comes from the hostel, and the boys like chanting for him and making him dance,' said Mandla.

'What was he doing when he was surrounded by the boys?'

'Do you really wish to know?'

'Yes. Is it a secret?'

'Come with me after school, and you'll find out.'

The man marched towards NY 1. He was a pitch-black man. His hair stood out in uncombed knots. Though he was wearing a municipal worker's overall, he did not look like a municipal worker at all. He was now perspiring heavily as the dancing became more and more intense. The crowd followed him up to the NY 1 junction of the road. He crossed NY 1 without even looking out for traffic and disappeared behind the hostels, still dancing and chanting, the crowd shouting behind him from across the street.

When he got back to the schoolyard, Gebashe met Naomi.

'Where have you been? I've been looking for you all over the place.'

'I was out in the street. We followed a madman.'

'Don't you know that we're not allowed on the streets during school hours? Lion wants to talk to us. He's in the staffroom.'

When they got to the staffroom, Lion gave them his bag and the books that he would be marking on the weekend to take to his house. Though Gebashe was still curious about the man he had seen that afternoon and though his curiosity was sharpened by Mandla's evasive answers to his questions, he had to postpone going with Mandla that day. Instead, he went with Naomi and spent the evening with Lion and his family.

CHAPTER 8

A crowd had gathered in NY 3A. A police informer was being stoned to death and set alight with petrol. The people were angry, and they wanted to wipe out all the informers in the township. Speech was in his room, reading a newspaper. Uncle Sam and his wife were seated in the lounge, not saying a word to each other. It was a Saturday afternoon, and the whole township was tense as the crowds burned buildings and cars.

Speech heard a timid knock at the door, and he invited whoever was knocking to come in. Naomi walked in timidly and sat on a chair near the door.

'Hello, Naomi! How did you manage to get through this turbulent street of ours?' asked Speech.

'I just walked on and avoided the crowd.'

'Yes, it is a hard time in our township. I understand you people burnt down a classroom yesterday?'

'Yes, we were on strike yesterday, and a classroom was burnt down.'

'What can I do for you, my little sister?'

'Lion has sent me to find out if Gebashe's at home.'

'I thought Gebashe spent last night at your home? He hasn't been here for three days. The last time I saw him, he was going to school on Thursday morning.'

'He wasn't at school on Thursday and yesterday. I last saw him on Wednesday afternoon after school. When I didn't see him on Thursday, I told Lion, and he said you might perhaps have detained him to do some urgent work for you.'

'No, Naomi, he didn't come home on Thursday, and then I thought Lion might have asked him to do a job for him. What could have happened to him?' asked Speech, rising to his feet.

'We don't know. Perhaps he may have run away from the riots.'

'No, it can't be. He has no money with him. Let me ask the people in the main house,' said Speech, going out swiftly.

After what seemed an eternity to Naomi, Speech returned, accompanied by Uncle Sam.

'You say he hasn't been to your house these past three days, Naomi?' asked Uncle Sam, having forgotten the courtesy of greeting the little girl first.

'No. I last saw him on Wednesday afternoon.'

'This is strange. How could he just disappear and to do so at such a dangerous time in the township!' said Uncle Sam in great bewilderment.

'What am I going to do? If anything happens to him, my father will kill me!' exclaimed Speech.

'Right now there is only one thing to do. Let's go and look for the boy. Naomi, you can go home and tell Lion that we have gone out to look for Gebashe.'

'I'll do that, Father. Goodbye,' said Naomi as she left swiftly but quietly.

'We'll take my car. Let's go to the police station first,' said Uncle Sam as soon as he was alone with Speech.

When they got to the Gugulethu Police Station, they found the place busy as usual. There were people reporting attacks, burglary, domestic violence, creditors, and all forms of violence. The policemen were taking down statements and locking people up in the cells. Speech and Uncle Sam filed in quietly and waited patiently for their turn to speak to the police at the reception.

'We are looking for a boy who disappeared on Thursday morning,' said Uncle Sam as soon as it was their turn to speak to the policeman.

'What's his name?' asked the policeman.

'Gebashe Nyaluza,' replied Uncle Sam.

Then the policeman looked through the case book, starting from Thursday's date. After a long and painful search, he said, 'No, we do not have any such name on our records. How old is he?'

'He's seventeen years old,' replied Speech.

'Do you have a photograph of him?'

'No. We didn't think of bringing one with us,' replied Uncle Sam regretfully.

'We need his photograph in order to identify him.'

'He doesn't have one. He is new in Cape Town,' said Speech.

'What was he wearing the last time you saw him?'

'A grey pair of trousers, a white shirt, and a Fezeka blazer.'

From the Gugulethu Police Station, they went to the Manenberg Police Station and then to Langa Police Station. In both these police stations, there was no trace of Gebashe.

'Now we must try the hospitals and then the mortuaries,' said Uncle Sam in despair.

They went to Somerset Hospital and, from there, to Groote Schuur Hospital and Tygerberg Hospital, but still there was no trace of Gebashe. Then they went to the police mortuary in Salt River. Here they had to look at bodies of unknown people. The place was haunted by death itself. There was blood on the floor, and the bodies that had been involved in accidents were still covered with blood. Had Speech been alone, he would not have even tried to look at the dead bodies. He was only encouraged by Uncle Sam's presence, but the sight of dead bodies killed his appetite for meat that day. They could not find Gebashe there either. So there was still hope that he could still be alive somewhere.

By this time, it was 8 p.m. and dangerous to be driving around in the township. But Speech and Uncle Sam decided to take the risk and see Lion in NY 75. When they got there, they found Lion and his family seated anxiously in the lounge. As they entered the lounge, they were hoping to find Gebashe there waiting for them. But there was no Gebashe to be found there and still no news of him.

'On Monday, I'll ask the children in his class, plus all his friends and teammates—those who'll manage to go to school,' said Lion.

'We'll come and find out what news you got,' said Uncle Sam as he and Speech stood up to go.

The following day was Sunday. Speech and Uncle Sam did not go to church. Instead, they went back to Lion's home to ask Naomi if she knew where Gebashe's friends lived. She knew where some of them lived, but when they got to their homes, they could not find Gebashe. Speech was worried about what his father would do when he found out that Gebashe was missing. He, Speech, had brought Gebashe to Cape Town against his father's wishes, and now Gebashe had disappeared.

On Monday afternoon, when Speech and Uncle Sam returned to Lion's home, they learnt that it was not Gebashe alone who was missing. Seven other boys from different homes were also missing. Nobody knew what had happened to them. Speech was a little comforted by the fact that a number of boys had disappeared together with Gebashe. At least there was hope that they were not dead but had gone somewhere—skipped the country perhaps? But how could he be sure? The police were capable of anything. If they found that these children were involved in riotous activities, they could easily torture them to death and bury them where no one would find them. But Gebashe was only a child. Moreover, he did not show interest in riots and anti-government protests. Gebashe was an ordinary country boy, and he was new to the city life.

The following day, Uncle Sam and Speech extended their search to relatives who lived at the hostels in Gugulethu and Langa, but without success. When they went to the families of the boys who had also disappeared, they could not find any clue. A week passed, and soon it became two weeks, but there was still no clue on Gebashe's disappearance. It was time for the writing of the end-of-the-year examinations at the schools. When it became clear that Gebashe would not come back and write the examinations, Speech became quite desperate. He would drive around the township, hoping to find Gebashe.

While he was on one of these daily investigations, he decided to go to the bus terminus, where there were buses to Transkei and Ciskei. Just as he was about to park his car, he saw a boy that looked like Gebashe, though his back was turned towards him as he started to board a bus.

'Gebashe! Gebashe! Gebashe!' shouted Speech as he pulled up the handbrake and switched off the ignition.

The boy did not seem to hear him and stepped inside the bus. Speech left his car without locking it and ran towards the bus. When he reached the bus, he got inside, and there was 'Gebashe' moving towards the back of the bus. Speech hurriedly pushed past a few people standing in the passage until he got behind 'Gebashe' and touched his shoulder, shouting, 'Gebashe! Gebashe!' Speech's heart sank when the blank face that turned round to look at him was that of a complete stranger.

Back at home, Uncle Sam and his wife were worried about Speech. They could see that the stress was taking its toll. He was restless and could not stay in one place for too long. What was worse was that he was often absent from work. Twice, the clerks from the municipal office came to look for him. Uncle Sam and his wife decided it was time to counsel him. He arrived late in the evening, and they called him to the main house.

'It is now the end of the second week since Gebashe disappeared, and we can see that this has a negative effect on you, Speech,' said Uncle Sam as soon as Speech had settled down.

'I-iya-a! Eish! I don't know what to do. I have looked everywhere in this township and in Langa without success,' said Speech, his arms looking like two majestic pillars supporting his head with his elbows on his knees.

'You dare not give up hope, Nozulu [Speech's clan name]. It will not be dark forever. There will soon be light at the end of the tunnel,' said MaNdlovu, Uncle Sam's wife.

'We have been thinking that it might be time for us to advise you to take it easy. My uncle, your father, will be angry right enough when he hears about this. It's natural. But he will not kill you for this. He is bound to understand that you have done everything in your power to find Gebashe,' said Uncle Sam, staring at the floor and not looking into Speech's eyes.

'My mother will be okay. But my father will not forgive me. Remember that my eldest sister, Gelesho, died while she was at a boarding school away from home. And now I took their last-born child and brought him to his death in Cape Town,' said Speech, also staring at the floor.

'Your father is an enlightened man, a teacher, and he understands that you wanted good education for your little brother,' said Uncle Sam.

'No, Bhuti Sam, my father does not understand why I brought Gebashe to Cape Town. You see, I stole Gebashe from Lehana, where he was doing his studies, and brought him to Cape Town without my father's permission. My father had flatly refused to let Gebashe come to Cape Town,' said Speech, tears rolling down his cheeks.

'Don't cry, my brother. We are in this together. But what you are telling us is quite shocking. We didn't know you brought Gebashe here without our uncle's permission. Well, it's too late to say it now, but you shouldn't have tried to give your little brother education without your father's blessings. Maybe that's why he's always faced with unfortunate situations. Do you remember how he narrowly escaped death last year? That should have given you a warning and a reason to come clean.'

'Now that's a serious matter! What are you going to do to appease my father-in-law?' exclaimed MaNdlovu.

'There is one thing remaining for us to do now. You and I must go home to Matatiele and tell my uncle and aunt the sad news,' said Uncle Sam with a decisive nod.

'Oh, my father! How are we going to breach the news to him?' said Speech as the supporting pillars collapsed and his head hung between his knees.

'It's been more than fifteen years since I was last seen at home in Matatiele, and I don't like the prospect of going there because I told myself long ago that I would never set foot there again. But for your sake, I am obliged to go against any vows that I may have made before. What do you say? Must we prepare to go?'

'Ye-es. I guess, there is no alternative. We must go and face my father.'

'The ancestors will look after us, and nothing will happen to us. I suggest that you take leave for the whole of next week, and we will leave this coming weekend. We'll use your car because it is relatively new compared to mine. Mine cannot take the journey in its present condition. Take your car in for a service, and MaNdlovu will prepare the provisions for us. What do you think?'

'Yes, it's fine. We can leave on Friday evening. We'll be at home on Saturday by midday.'

'It's a good thing that both of you are going. Haven't you already written a letter informing them at home about this?' asked MaNdlovu.

'No, I haven't. I couldn't steel myself to write to my father, especially after the way I took Gebashe from home. My father wrote me a letter declaring that I must never again set foot at home.'

'Let us hope that our uncle will find it in his heart to forgive you. Poor Speech . . . I'm glad, Tata, that you are accompanying Speech to his home. The ancestors will indeed give you their blessings,' said MaNdlovu to her husband.

So the preparations started for the eighteen-hour journey to KwaKhesa, Matatiele. Uncle Sam was what was called an *itshipha* in the rural areas—a person who abandons his home in the rural areas and comes to live in a city for the rest of his life. But staying with his cousin Speech rekindled the desire for him to go back home. He used to ask Speech about all those people he grew up with and about the old men in the family. He would then tell Speech stories about the things they did when they were growing up. Uncle Sam's grandfather and Speech's grandfather were brothers.

Speech had discovered the whereabouts of Samuel when he started working for the City Council as a storeman. One of the municipal workers had asked Speech if he knew Mr Nyaluza of NY 3A when he learnt that he was also a Nyaluza. He replied that he did not know him, but if the worker said he was of the same Khesa clan as himself, he would like to meet him. The meeting was then arranged, and that was how the two cousins discovered each other.

Samuel was fifty years old and working as a carpenter for the municipality. Speech had been twenty-six years of age when he came to live with Samuel. There was a big gap in age between Speech and Gebashe as the latter was born when his parents already thought they were past the stage of having a baby. For this reason, Gebashe grew up as a spoilt child dearly loved by both his parents. When his school performance proved to be excellent, he became even more spoilt, in the opinion of the elder children.

CHAPTER 9

Uncle Sam and Speech left Gugulethu at 5 p.m., and on the N1, they joined the stream of traffic mostly of people coming from work in the city. By 5.40 p.m., they were going past Paarl. Speech was behind the wheel of his Land Rover. When they reached Laingsburg, they took a break to obtain petrol. In Beaufort West, Uncle Sam took over the wheel to face the stretch of road from Beaufort West to Aberdeen. At Middleburg, Uncle Sam gave the wheel to Speech. Both men had not slept a wink throughout the night, their eyes following what seemed to be an endless road. They drove on past Elliot, Ugie, Maclear. When they reached Mount Fletcher, they began to relax because that would be the last urban settlement they would pass before arriving home. It was now about 10 a.m.

By twelve midday, Speech's Land Rover stood at the gate of his home. When he got out to open the gate, the dogs came running and barking. Dogs never forget. Even if a person has been away for a year, they can still recognize him. They now immediately recognized Speech and started wagging their tails and coming to sniff at him.

Hearing the dogs barking, Khubelo went out to investigate. When she saw her brother's Land Rover, she immediately withdrew into the hut to tell her mother that Speech was at the gate. Instead of joy, the two women were

63

gripped with fear, wondering what brought Speech here without first telling them he was coming home. Instinctively, the two women knew there was something wrong. They waited anxiously for Speech to come in.

'Greetings, Mother! Greetings, Sisi!' said Speech at the door.

'Greetings, my son! We didn't expect to see you!' said Sarah as she shook hands with Speech and Uncle Sam. 'I think I know you. Aren't you a child of the family?' said Sarah as she took Uncle Sam's hand into both her hands.

'Yes, Mother, it's Samuel.'

'Oh, Samuel! We nearly didn't see you until we went to our graves. How are you, my son?'

'I'm fine, Mother. I'm still alive.'

'Your mother and father will be very glad indeed. They have now aged, and your father's eyesight has deteriorated badly.'

After the formalities of greeting, the two men sat on benches against the wall, and the two women sat on a mat opposite them next to the fireplace.

'Where's Father, Mother?' asked Speech.

'He went to an imbizo [meeting] at the chief's place at Lukholweni. He will be away the whole day. After the imbizo, he will visit the agricultural demonstrator to get advice as it is the growing season.'

'We have come to speak to you and Father. We are here about Gebashe. He is missing, and we don't know where he is.'

'Oh, my child! What news is this that you are bringing us now! How did this happen?'

'He left for school in the morning of a Thursday about three weeks ago and never came back. We have looked everywhere in Gugulethu and Langa, at the police stations, hospitals, mortuaries. He is just nowhere to be found. He simply disappeared. We were hoping against hope that he might be here.'

'No, he didn't come here, my child. Speech! What's your father going to say about this? How are we going to tell him? Only yesterday, he was talking about how you disobeyed him. Now what is he going to say?'

'We don't know what Father's going to say, Mother. That is why Bhuti Samuel decided to come with me.'

'Oh, my poor baby Gebashe! What are we going to do? How could this happen to us after we lost Gelesho? People don't want my children to be educated!'

'Calm down, Mother. You know this is not good for your health,' said Khubelo quietly.

'I'm so sorry, Mother, that this has happened,' said Uncle Sam. 'But there are seven other boys missing from the school where he is a learner. We think that Gebashe isn't alone in this.'

'What did they say at his school?' asked Khubelo.

'At his school, they don't know what happened. They are as puzzled as we are by this.'

Sarah started crying softly, and Khubelo hugged her and tried to comfort her. The men held their heads in their hands and fell silent. Everyone in the room was heartbroken. They all dreaded the encounter with Speech's father in the evening. When Speech's mother finally calmed down, it was decided that Speech and Uncle Sam should visit Uncle Sam's parents at his home while they waited for the return of Meshack from Lukholweni. The reunion between Samuel and his family was the only positive part of this visit. Also it was a good excuse for postponing the meeting with Speech's father.

In the evening, they started their long wait for Speech's father to come home. They had their meals quietly. Now the rest of the family was home. Khaya had returned with the cattle, and he was delighted to see Speech. He did not know Uncle Sam at all. Everybody was enjoying the provisions that had come with Speech and Uncle Sam. At 9 p.m., they heard Mbulunga's hooves as the horse arrived with its master. Khaya ran outside to remove the saddle and to lead the horse to its meal. This was Khaya's duty whenever Meshack arrived on horseback. As always, Meshack had been drinking and was in an aggressive mood.

'How can you be here alone? Where's my child?' asked Meshack after recognizing Speech and refusing to shake hands with him.

'Do you know who I've got here, Father?' asked Speech by way of avoiding the earlier question from his father.

'No, I don't. Who's this?'

'It's Samuel, Father,' said Uncle Sam politely.

'Samuel! I think I know that name! Is it my cousin Foloti's son?'

'Yes, Father, the one and only son.'

'Oh, my son! So you've come home at last? Home is home, my son. No one will change that.'

'Yes, Father, it's true. Home is home indeed. Here I am today.'

When drunk, Meshack had the tendency to talk endlessly, not giving other people a chance to respond. So now he started relating how Samuel grew up, the things he did as a child, special incidents, and the names of his father's cows.

'Father, we are here about something serious,' said Speech, taking advantage of a brief pause in his father's endless talk. 'Gebashe is missing . . . and we don't know where he is.'

There was a long silence after that. No one could guess if Meshack had heard what Speech had just said. In a moment, Meshack turned round and stared at his son without blinking.

Finally, he said slowly, 'Did you speak about Gebashe?'

'Yes, Father, Gebashe's missing. We don't know where he is.'

'Do you come here to tell me a fairy tale after abducting my child and taking him to Cape Town against my wishes!'

'I'm sorry, Father' was all Speech could manage to say.

'Is this why you brought Samuel here? To show us the ways of the city that he has taught you?' said Meshack, suddenly standing up. 'Go! Go and find Gebashe. Find him and bring him to me!'

An idea occurred to Uncle Sam, and he said, 'We think that these boys have been recruited by the freedom fighters, Father. Seven other boys are missing with him. If that is the case, then Gebashe is out of the country.'

'Ha, Samuel! Have you taught my children to do *poqo* [PAC slogan]? Have you taught them to disobey me and to do what they like?'

'Father! Please, Father! Please, Nozulu! Just hear us,' said Speech in desperation.

'I said go! And never come back to my house without my child! I said go, and I'm not going to repeat that!'

'Can't you please, please listen to your son, titshala!' pleaded Sarah, already on her feet. Everybody in the room was on his or her feet, even the children.

'You shut up! You are just a woman. That's what you are! Speech, I said leave my house and never come back here without Gebashe!'

And so it was that Speech took his belongings and spent the night at Uncle Sam's home. On Sunday, Speech and Uncle Sam again attempted to talk to Meshack, hoping that now that he was sober, he would listen to them. But he was worse than the previous night. Finally, they gave up and went back to Uncle Sam's home to prepare for their journey back to Cape Town.

Speech left his home with a heavy heart. He did not know if he would ever again see his family, his mother, and siblings, let alone his father, who did not want to even look at him. It was a sad day for Speech's mother. To lose both her sons was unbearable. She pleaded with her husband to forgive Speech, but instead, he threatened to beat her up if she continued to nag him.

Early on Tuesday morning, Speech and Uncle Sam arrived at No. 20 NY 3A. They were exhausted from their long journey, but more than that, they were both depressed by the results of their journey to KwaKhesa. Speech could not come to terms with the fact that he had been thrown out of his home by his own father. Once, Uncle Sam found him standing in the street in front of the house, calling, 'Geba-a-she! Geba-a-she! Geba-a-she!' It was then that Uncle Sam advised Speech to see a medicine man. The disappearance of his little brother was having a negative effect on his health.

Indeed, on the Saturday of the week in which they had returned from home, they went to see Nondala, a medicine man known to Uncle Sam. He made incisions on Speech's joints and applied some medicine. Then he gave him a bottle of medicine to take home, and he was supposed to take a spoonful in the morning and in the evening.

'Do you really think Gebashe has been recruited?' Speech asked Uncle Sam on their way home from the medicine man.

'It just occurred to me when I spoke to your father. I really do not know what to think. Everything is possible,' replied Uncle Sam.

'What you said actually made sense. The very fact that not only Gebashe but seven other boys have disappeared makes me wonder if it's not perhaps the ANC. My father was angry with me, but what he said about poqo opened my eyes. Ever since that utterance, I have been thinking and hoping that Gebashe has skipped the country.'

'But at his age, what could he do against the white people? And what's even more puzzling is that he is new to these things. He comes from the rural areas and knows nothing about freedom fighting.'

'Well, whatever the motive, there is yet hope for us,' concluded Speech.

For the first time ever since he came to Cape Town, Speech did not go home to KwaKhesa for his holidays. He had sent money to his fiancée so that she could come and join him in Cape Town and they could get married. The marriage vows were exchanged between Speech and Nomsa in a government office in December; Uncle Sam and his wife, MaNdlovu, acted as witnesses. Thereafter, there was no party, no honeymoon—nothing. Nomsa came from the Mashiya clan at Lukholweni. For her, coming to Cape Town was the beginning of years of playing hide-and-seek with the influx control officials until she got a pass to live in Gugulethu.

Chapter 10

After the unbanning of political parties, there was an influx of black South Africans coming home from exile. Speech waited to hear news of Gebashe, but there was no news. After Mandla, one of the boys who had disappeared at the same time as Gebashe, wrote a letter to his family to tell them he lived in Zambia, Speech's hope was rekindled. Lion had brought the letter to Speech after Mandla's parents gave it to him. Speech waited and hoped his brother would write to him a line or two, but nothing like that happened.

There they were—Mandla's parents, his sister Sisanda, Lion, and Speech—at D. F. Malan Airport to welcome Mandla home. Speech was hoping against hope that Gebashe would be there too. But when Mandla appeared at the arrivals gate, he was alone with his family—his wife, Zanele, and three kids. There were all the excitement of a reunion and all that joy. But it all created a heavy sadness in Speech's heart. He wished Gebashe was still alive and would come back to him to be his ticket to his father's heart.

Rejected by his father and expelled from his family, he was a lost man. He now had a family of his own and had bought himself a house of his own in the township. He had two kids, both of them at a technical college. But without his mother, father, siblings, and cousins, he was a lost soul. His children, Ayanda and Mvumeni, had never seen their grandparents. And the news that his parents were now quite old and troubled by ill health brought no comfort to him. But every time he thought about home, his mind played back his father's fury.

Speech waited until all the excitement of Mandla's arrival died down, which meant that he had to return to Mandla's home the following day. Mandla was his last hope. If he said he did not know what happened to Gebashe, then all was lost, and he and his wife and children would be swallowed up by the city. It would destroy the last glitter of hope of ever coming together with his brother again. He did not even go to Uncle Sam so that he could come and be with him when he heard the news. He just wanted to be alone when he heard whatever Mandla had to tell him.

The following day, he waited until late in the afternoon. He did not want to show Mandla how anxious he was. When he arrived at Mandla's home, he was told that Mandla had left that morning for a meeting in Montana. They were preparing for the first democratic elections in SA. He left a message for Mandla to phone him and arrange a meeting.

Arranging an appointment with a politician is a difficult process. You leave your phone number, and he never phones back. You phone him, and he never takes your call but someone else; a secretary answers the phone. When he finally comes to the phone, he tells you he is busy right now and that he will call you back in an hour's time; then an hour passes by, and he never calls. In those days, there were no cellular phones in SA. Today, you call his cell number, and you hit a voicemail.

So Speech did not find the opportunity to ask Mandla if Gebashe was with him when he left the country. Speech was now getting desperate.

Then he met Lion at the shopping centre in Ottery. Lion mentioned in passing that there was going to be a welcome-home party for Mandla at his home in Gugulethu.

'Oh, when is his welcome-home party?' asked Speech.

'This coming Saturday. Have you had a chance to find out from him about Gebashe?' asked Lion.

'No, this man is so busy with his freedom politics. I must nail him down at this party.'

At Mandla's party, there were people from exile, ex-prisoners from Robben Island, and activists from various organizations. Speech got his chance when Mandla got up to wander through the crowd after all the speeches and formalities.

'Excuse me, Mr Moni. My name is Speech Nyaluza. I am the one that has been phoning you for an appointment. I have been wondering if, when you left the country, my brother, Gebashe Nyaluza, was with you,' said Speech.

'Sorry, Mr Nyaluza. We are not allowed to discuss operations of the organization with the public,' said Mandla as he turned around to walk away.

'I just want to know if Gebashe's still alive, that's all,' said Speech. But Mandla had already turned his back on him and was busy talking to other people. That was it. After all the pains he had taken to meet this man, Speech was now being snubbed and called 'the public' by a fellow black South African, fellow sufferer, fellow Xhosa.

If he had not been in exile or in prison for politics, he would have been a nonentity. Since when did running away from home, running away from family, and leaving the enemy to do what he liked with your people—since when did this create heroes? 'Did I see you in Lusaka?' was the password for these fellows. Otherwise, they did not see you even while looking at you.

Speech gave up and went home, disheartened and angry.

'I have never been so humiliated and angry. He just walked away from me,' said Speech while telling Uncle Sam about his recent experience.

'Let's wait until things calm down. We must go back to him,' said Uncle Sam.

'I bet he knows something about Gebashe. Why else would he talk about operations of the organization when I ask him about my brother?'

'He knows something, all right. Where there's smoke, there's fire.'

As it happened, things never calmed down for Mandla. With the coming of the elections, he became a member of parliament and left the township to live in a suburb. So Speech could not learn the simple truth about whether his brother, Gebashe, had skipped the country or not. Most people were back in the country by this time. Even the bones of those who died in exile were returned to the country. But there was no sign of Gebashe.

Speech reluctantly came to the conclusion that he must have been murdered by the police's special branch and buried secretly somewhere in Cape Town. Uncle Sam agreed with him that Gebashe was dead and buried where they could not find him. What Speech wanted to do now was to try and make peace with his father. He had acted irresponsibly to bring Gebashe to Cape Town without his father's permission.

It was time for him to face the consequences of his actions and humble himself before his father. His parents were quite old and might die without giving him, his wife, and his children any blessings.

He mentioned this to Uncle Sam, and they both agreed that it was time for Speech to visit the old man despite the fact that his father had said in expelling him from home that he must never come back without Gebashe. It would have been much better if he returned with Gebashe's bones. It was exactly for that reason that Speech kept postponing his visit home though he had agreed that the time for it was right. He had caused his parents so much pain that coming back to them empty-handed seemed to him not quite right.

Naomi was now a lawyer at Brian Austin and Associates in Cape Town. She had done all her studies at Fezeka, which soon became a high school in her time. After Fezeka, she was admitted for a BA degree at the University of Cape Town. Her matriculation symbols were quite good and enabled her to get a place in the Faculty of Arts. She was the first person in her family to study for a degree. Lion had gone up to matriculation, which was a high qualification and a great achievement in his time, and thereafter, he did a teachers' course. It took Naomi four years to finish her degree because of the quality of her basic education, which was poor compared to the education in the whites' schools. That she actually completed her degree was a great achievement for her as other students either took longer or failed to complete altogether.

While still at high school, Naomi never had a boyfriend. She had been so attached to Gebashe that though love was never mentioned between them, she felt she owed it to him even when he was missing to remain without a boyfriend. It was mainly because they were still young and also because their brothers treated each other as relatives that they had regarded each other as brother and sister. Though it was clear from childhood that Naomi would grow up to be a beautiful woman, Gebashe never saw her as anything beyond a sister, and so was the case with her.

At UCT, she was at her full bloom, and young men were quite attracted to her. Also, as years went by, she began to accept that Gebashe was lost to her forever. So she fell in love with a student from Natal. His name was Zama Khumalo. Zama was ahead of her by a year. When he finished his BA, he registered for an LLB degree. In this way, he influenced his girlfriend, who also took LLB as soon as she finished her BA degree.

It was while they were doing their LLB that the talk of getting married occurred between them. Then Naomi stopped using contraceptives, and soon she was pregnant. Virginity is no longer a subject of pride with the young women of today. What they like more than anything is having a child to prove that the relationship is successful. Also, the parents of today do not make the demands that parents in the past used to make when their daughters fell pregnant.

Naomi's father had passed away, and only her mother was left behind. When she heard of her daughter's pregnancy, she left the whole matter to her eldest son, Lion, and his sister to sort out. On his part, Lion wanted to be flexible about the whole thing and to do only what his sister suggested should be done. As it is, she suggested that nothing should be done. She loved her child's father, and they were going to get married.

Time went by, but Zama did not finally commit himself to marriage. He supported Naomi when the child was born, and they began to live together in a flat. At the end of four years, Zama finished his LLB and went back home to practise as a lawyer. He continued to support his daughter but kept postponing the marriage. Naomi also finished her LLB and joined Brian Austin and Associates, a legal firm in Cape Town.

CHAPTER 11

The telephone in Naomi's office rang.

'Hello!'

'Is this Brian Austin and Associates?'

'Yes, that's correct.'

'May I speak to Naomi Noyanda please?'

'Naomi speaking.'

'Oh, hi, Naomi! How are you?'

'I'm fine, thanks. And you?'

'I'm also fine. It's been a long time.'

'A long time for what? Who am I speaking to?' asked Naomi, rather irritated by this voice whose owner seemed to assume that he was well-known to her.

'You're speaking to Mandla.'

'Mandla who?'

'Mandla Moni, Gebashe's friend. We were together at Fezeka.'

'What! Am I speaking to the great man himself? You must be joking, Mr Moni.'

'Come on, Naomi, since when have I stopped being your former schoolmate? I would like to talk to you about Gebashe. The last I heard of him, he was in Mbabane, Swaziland.'

'Are you sure? How long ago did you last see him?'

'Roughly fifteen years. After matriculating in Tanzania, we went our separate ways, and I never saw him ever since.'

'Wow, that's great news! At least now we've got a lead. What made you change your mind? I understand you didn't want to tell his brother where he was.'

'Gebashe always talked about you. He had great ideas about what you and he would do when he came back home. Then someone spread the propaganda that some of our comrades had turned their backs on the struggle and returned back to South Africa. His name was mentioned among these comrades. But when I came back, I verified that no such thing had happened. So when his brother spoke to me, I didn't have the facts just yet.'

'Thixo wamazulu! [God of heaven!] It must have been very tough for all of you out there.'

'I couldn't jeopardize the operations of the organization. Anyway, the first person I wanted to talk to was you as soon as I had all the facts verified. So I got your contact details.'

'Why did you still not communicate with his brother?'

'I'd actually like you to call him and tell him what I've just told you.'

'Ha-a! Ha-a! Ha-a! Gebashe! Could it be that all this time he is in Swaziland?' said Naomi after an uncertain pause.

Immediately after putting down the phone, Naomi called her brother, Lion. He was now teaching at Gugulethu School of Commerce.

'Hello, Bhuti! You will not believe what I'm going to tell you. I have been talking to Mandla Moni on the phone a few minutes ago!'

'That's great! What does he want?'

'He says that Gebashe could be in Swaziland.'

'Then why didn't he come home when they got their freedom?'

'Mandla does not know the answer to that question either. He says he last saw Gebashe about fifteen years ago.'

'I'm leaving everything right now. I'm going to tell his brother the news. Do you know if perhaps Mandla has been in touch with him?'

'Mandla hasn't contacted Gebashe's brother yet. That's why I'm phoning. I was the first to learn. Please give Bhut' Speech Mandla's contact details.'

Lion and Speech were great friends now. They spent weekends together watching soccer on TV. Speech was now a director at the municipal offices, and Lion was deputy principal. On months' ends, their families would come together for braais. Lion gave Speech a call to make sure that he was in his office and told him that he was coming over because there was something he wanted to discuss with him. Then he got into his car and drove to the Civic Centre.

'What's wrong, Lion? Why could you not just talk on the phone?' asked Speech as soon as Lion got into his office.

'I have important news for you. Here is Mandla's phone number. Call him. He thinks Gebashe lives in Swaziland.'

'Can it be true? Gebashe is in Swaziland?'

When Speech and Lion arrived in Mbabane, they went to the Home Affairs office to make their initial enquiry. The Home Affairs office had the name of a Dr Nyaluza who had a surgery in town. He was a Swazi citizen originally from South Africa. They were given the telephone number of the surgery, and as soon as they left the office, they looked for public telephones in order to call the surgery. They were both tense and anxious, praying that this Dr Nyaluza was the person they were looking for.

'Just dial the number, Nozulu, and ask whom you're talking to,' said Lion.

Speech dialled with a nervous finger the number given to him by Lion. After ringing for some seconds, someone picked up the phone. A lady's voice said, 'Doctor's surgery. How may I help you?'

Speech was not sure what to say next. 'Did you say doctor's surgery?'

'Yes. Dr Nyaluza's surgery. Can I help you?'

When Speech heard the surname, he thought that perhaps he should ask to speak to Dr Nyaluza. So he said, 'May I speak to Dr Nyaluza please?'

'Who do I say is calling?'

'My name is Speech Nyaluza.'

'Please hold on.'

There was a pause, and a male voice said, 'Dr Nyaluza. Hello.'

'This is Speech Nyaluza. Whom am I talking to?'

There was a long pause, and then the voice on the other side said, 'This is Gebashe.'

There was another long pause before Speech said, 'Are you my long-lost brother, Gebashe?'

'Yes, Nozulu! How did you find my number?'

'From the Home Affairs office here in Mbabane. We are here in Mbabane. I'm with Lion.'

Lion stood patiently as this conversation took place. Speech and Gebashe talked for more than thirty minutes. And when he put down the telephone, he went to Lion, and the two men hugged each other. Both were in tears, and for both of them, this was not the time for words. They stood there in an iron embrace, oblivious to what was going on in the streets of Mbabane.

At first, Naomi was so excited that Gebashe had at last been found. But then, as she thought about all that had happened between them—the riots, the protest marches, the other men and women that had become part of their lives, their careers—her heart sank to the bottom. She looked at her love life; it was in shambles. Her daughter was now seven years old, and she, Naomi, could get married any day now. Though she had not asked Gebashe, she knew instinctively that even if he was single, there was a woman in his life too and probably children as well.

These were all the inheritance they got from apartheid— first, broken families, then loveless lives and empty careers that isolated them even more from the community. Gebashe's homecoming would be nothing but a series of painful episodes of unrequited love. Without doubt, she was happy he had been found at last, but alas, she could not feature in his life, and he could not feature in hers either.

Should she then allow herself to enter into a marriage of convenience with Zama? What if Gebashe was still available? What would happen to her daughter? These questions had no direct answers, and they assailed Naomi's thoughts without relief. There was nothing she could do with the way she was—a career woman who was socially alienated. She could not rewind and start from the beginning.

What made things worse was that Zama called her that very afternoon she had received the news of Gebashe from Lion in Mbabane. He wanted a date on which his people could come and pay lobola.

'Can this wait just a little more? There's something I need to sort out first,' said Naomi on the phone.

'But, sweetie, this has waited long enough. Isn't this what we've both been dreaming of?'

'Yes, darling, it's our dream, but we have waited for a long time already. A few more weeks will not matter.'

Gebashe lived in a big house on the outskirts of town. The house was owned by Mrs Vilakazi, a prominent businesswoman whose husband had died of malaria early in their marriage. She had inherited her father's business when the latter died as well as her husband's business. Her father had been a fruit-and-vegetable merchant while her husband had owned a clothing business. Her house was full because she lived with her mother as well as several uncles and aunts, plus her children and the children of relatives. The way things were, she seemed to possess everything—house, cars, vans, trucks, businesses, relatives, and even a husband. It was Gebashe who now played this role of her husband.

On the evening of Speech and Lion's arrival, Gebashe was the first to come home.

'Gebashe, we've come to ask you to return to South Africa, to come home with us,' said Speech as soon as they got a chance to be alone with Gebashe.

'I hear you, my brother, but I'm happy in Swaziland. Here I am treated as a human being, and I live a full life as a respectable professional. You may have done away with apartheid at home, but it will take generations for the mindset to change. I had decided that I would never see home again,' said Gebashe, his head hanging between his knees.

'But, Nozulu, you have a community to develop and a country to build. Swaziland does not need you as much as we do,' said Lion in a sombre voice.

'More than this, there is the problem of Noni, my wife. When the news of South Africa's freedom came, she stressed that if ever I thought of going home, I would do so without her. She would never leave her businesses and come home with me.'

'Things have changed now at home. We must talk to her and see what she says,' said Speech with much emphasis.

'I'll leave it to you both to convince her. But I must warn you, when she has made up her mind, no one can change her. Women in this country are independent and free,' said Gebashe, rising to go and talk to someone in the front hall.

Noni arrived after eight in the evening, after her businesses had closed for the day. She was a loud-spoken woman, and she started calling out loudly while she was still in the garage. She wanted the servants and children to come and take the things in plastic bags from her car. She was strongly built, and toughness was written all over her. When she was introduced to the visitors by her husband, her face did not register any emotion. The moment they saw her, Speech and Lion were convinced that Gebashe was right and that it would be an uphill battle to make her change her mind about South Africa. So they decided to postpone the consultation to a future date.

Noni continued to ignore the visitors, and it was clear from Gebashe's gloomy look that he was having serious talks with his wife. This made Speech and Lion quite uneasy about her. On the third day, the two men approached

Gebashe when he returned from work and asked him if he had discussed returning home with his wife.

'The moment Noni saw you, she knew what your mission was and accused me of bringing you here,' said Gebashe in response.

'It is quite evident from the way she looks at us that she does not like us at all,' said Lion.

'How do you keep up with such a raw woman, Nozulu? I dare say she's quite a personality,' said Speech.

'You may be right. She's the boss around here, and her word is final. But then we fell in love with each other, and now we're married.'

'We must talk to both of you this evening. We can't stay here indefinitely, not knowing if you're coming home with us or not. In any case, what is *your* feeling about coming home with us?' asked Lion.

'Though I had decided to settle down permanently in Swaziland, I don't mind coming to South Africa with you if my family agrees to come with me. As I said earlier, I'm happy here. Life's good to me,' replied Gebashe in a sombre note.

'What about our mom and dad? They have aged, Gebashe, and are about to die,' said Speech.

'I'm not lying when I say I really miss them. And I say again, I'm sorry about what I've put you through,' replied Gebashe.

When Noni arrived, all four of them gathered in the private lounge, and Lion introduced the subject of Gebashe and his family moving with them to South Africa. Throughout Lion's speech, Noni sat upright and tense, paying attention to every detail.

When Lion had finished speaking, she bent forward, looked him up and down, and said, 'To start with, I must tell you, mister, that I'm only doing you a favour in speaking to you. Here in Mbabane, we have never seen people from Gebashe's family in South Africa. My people have never negotiated my marriage to Gebashe with your people. So there is no contract in the form of cattle or money or anything between my clan and your clan. Gebashe's marriage to me is purely a contract between the two of us, and right from the start, we agreed that there would be no talk of relocating to South Africa at any stage of our marriage. Can you imagine me dehumanising myself and living as a disadvantaged black woman in a strike-torn country like South Africa!'

'Yes, you may be right about a strike-torn country. But things have changed in South Africa. We got our freedom, which we had been fighting for, and—' Before Lion could finish what he was saying, she broke in.

'Don't tell me about freedom from your white government! You had a negotiated settlement, and what does that mean? It means that you will be perpetually dominated by rich white people. It means that you will be perpetually poor and disadvantaged. You will continue to be the underdogs in your own country. Right now you are spreading a myth about economic freedom. Freedom is freedom. There's no economic freedom, social freedom, or whatever colour freedom! Soon you will be asking for freedom to have toilets and to use them!'

Noni's arrogance was quite annoying to the two men, and Speech said quite angrily, 'So you think you are better off than us in South Africa? Let me tell you something! The

South African social set-up is changing fast, and soon all our people will enjoy the fruits of freedom.'

Upon this, Noni turned, looked directly into Speech's face, and said, 'Tell me, my man, who is changing South Africa's social set-up? Is it the corrupt government officials?'

'We are not all corrupt. Some of us are working hard to effect changes in the lives of people and—'

'Can you tell me what changes you have successfully effected so far?' Noni asked, looking defiantly at Speech.

'Whoa! Whoa! Whoa! This argument is not taking us anywhere. Can we all please calm down and speak with respect to one another?' said Gebashe, lifting his hands in the air.

'Are you saying I must calm down and allow these people to break up my marriage? Is that what you want?' said Noni, facing her husband.

'If you must behave so arrogantly, then we don't need you in SA. Let Gebashe come home with us, and we'll ask nothing of you.'

'You are disgusting! You come all the way from South Africa, and you want me to listen to this nonsense! You two, get out of my house—now!' said Noni, rising to her feet and pointing at the door.

Everybody now stood up, and they all spoke at the same time, insulting each other and calling each other names. Quite shaken by the confrontation, Speech and Lion packed their bags and left for a hotel.

Before they parted from Gebashe, Lion said to him, 'Nozulu, be careful of this woman. She would poison you if she had to. I'm giving up. I can't convince her. She hates

South Africa with all her heart and soul. But I warn you. Be careful of her.'

The following day, Speech and Lion were in a plane bound for Johannesburg.

Every time Gebashe thought of home, the picture of his parents and his siblings and cousins kept nagging him. When he thought of Cape Town, Naomi was foremost in his mind. The bond that had developed between them was something that not even distance could eliminate. Like Naomi, he had told himself that though he had no claim to her, she was the only woman in his life. When he was at high school in Tanzania, he had a girlfriend, but she was just for whiling away the time. In his heart of hearts, he had resolved to marry Naomi the moment he returned home.

The political situation in his country had snapped the bonds between individuals, their families, and their loved ones. While in Cuba, he broke ties with Lillian, his Tanzanian girlfriend, and continued without a girlfriend. It was not until he came to practise as a doctor in Swaziland that he got involved with a woman. He and Noni decided to marry. The bond was more profession-driven than love-fuelled. They respected each other, but the subject of returning to SA was always a sore point between them. Gebashe could only blame apartheid for being displaced so that he found himself with a family consisting of the wrong wife.

It was a month after Speech and Lion returned to Cape Town that Speech received a call from Gebashe. The latter was saying that life in his family had become unbearable. He had moved to a bachelor flat and was suing for divorce. He was coming home. Despite the tragic events, this was indeed good news.

CHAPTER 12

Preparations to bring Gebashe back to Cape Town got under way. Naomi was also involved in the preparations. The ANC secured a house in Parow. Meanwhile, Zama pressed for marriage. Naomi tried all the delaying tactics she could manage, but he persisted. When he saw that she was now reluctant to marry him, he sensed that there could be another man in her life. When he asked her, she denied this, but he was not sure whether to trust her or not. Then he approached Lion, but the latter's response was that he must talk to his fiancée.

For Speech, the remaining days in the countdown for his reunion with his brother appeared to be going slower than usual. Speech had now bought himself a house in Montana. That was where Gebashe's welcome-home party would be. Once again, they would be rubbing shoulders with prominent ANC leaders and politicians. Uncle Sam and his family bought presents, and Lion was responsible for the programme of the day. Speech asked Naomi to be one of the speakers, but she politely refused, stating that she would be too shy to speak in the presence of Gebashe.

Speech and Uncle Sam invited all the members of the Nyaluza family who worked in Cape Town to form a family council. All the members of the family council had to observe secrecy. Gebashe's return was not to reach

KwaKhesa just yet. They had planning meetings held in Uncle Sam's house. The first thing to organize was a party on the day of Gebashe's arrival. Then there would be a welcome-home party on a Saturday a week after his arrival.

They were to buy live sheep and an ox from one of the farms in Philippi for the two occasions—four hamels for the arrival party and eight sheep and an ox for the welcome-home party. In the black township, people do not go to the butchery to buy meat for a big occasion—a wedding or a funeral. They buy live animals which they slaughter themselves in their own traditional way.

There was to be alcohol—beer, brandy, whisky. But more than that, the women were going to prepare traditional beer from corn. This beer, though it is drunk by the elders, is in reality food for the ancestors, and an important occasion like this was to be dedicated to the ancestors. On the ANC side, Mandla and the local cadres liaised with the family council and helped Lion design the programme.

The day of Gebashe's arrival in Cape Town was a rainy winter day. This was fitting because rain is a blessing for the Nozulu clan. As soon as he appeared at the arrival gate, he was greeted by a large banner written with 'Welcome home, Gebashe'. He immediately raised his fist in saluting the crowd. He was now a fully grown man, tall like his father, and with large bones. The moment the crowd set eyes on him, the men started to sing his praises, and the women ululated.

The praise poet moved forward, saying the praises of Gebashe's clan:

> It is Gebashe, the name;
> it is Gebashe, the clan name.

He is Khesa; he is Nozulu.
He is the weather:
sometimes it's clear;
sometimes it's overcast.
But it's raining today
because the ancestors are smiling.
He is the one that soars high in the sky,
a Nguni who comes home fresh and clean
like corn stalks in autumn,
offspring of the woman with long breasts,
who stretched them to feed the baby
across the Buffalo and the Tugela rivers.
He's the persistent one
who endeavoured to dwell
on the slopes of the Mjomla Mountain
until pigweed grew thereon,
the burweed and euphorbia bush
which they try to chop down
but it makes their axes blunt.

Then the crowd burst into a freedom song.

Leader: UTamb' ukweziya nta-aba. [Tambo is on those
         mountains.]
Chorus: Uman' uman' ugiji-ima. [Keep running.]
Leader: Giji-ima nawe, comrade. [You too keep running,
         comrade.]
Chorus: Uman' uman' ugiji-ima.
Leader: Giji-ima nawe, comrade.

When Gebashe reached the crowd, he fell into the embrace of his brother, Speech. Thereafter, everyone wanted to hold him. Naomi was standing shyly with three other young women at the back of the crowd. Gebashe recognized her without anybody's help. They locked into a long embrace without saying a word.

At long last, Gebashe spoke first, 'Here I am, Naomi. You're the main reason I'm home today!'

'Welcome home, Gebashe! I'm so glad you are here!' she managed to say.

That night, only the little children went to sleep. Everybody else remained awake until the following day. There was no time for intimate talk between Gebashe and Naomi. They saw each other from a distance as everyone wanted to talk to Gebashe—the family members, his former teachers, his former fellow learners, the comrades, and politicians. The son of the soil was back home to his roots. The ANC planned an endless schedule of visits, which included a visit to President Mandela's official residence, Genadendal in Rondebosch.

For Gebashe, seeing Mandela, his leader, face to face was an unforgettable experience. Madiba had said to him, 'Welcome home, Comrade Nyaluza. As you can see, we now have a country to build. Put on your overalls, comrade, and start working. There's no time to spare. The time for suffering in the hands of an illegitimate government is now over. Our uniting slogan says there's always tomorrow.'

The welcome-home party was another big event. The slaughtering of an ox marked the traditional significance of the occasion. Other comrades, most of whom were now members of parliament and ministers of the Mandela government, spoke at the occasion, and the celebrations were at fever pitch. Gebashe was so busy with meetings that he hardly found time to speak to Naomi.

It appeared, however, that Naomi was avoiding speaking to him. Every time, she would greet him, and before he could say anything, she would say, 'I know you're busy catching up. I'm not going to detain you. See you later.'

The poor girl had decided the moment she set eyes on him at the airport that he was too good—too full of glory—for her. He was a hero and a patriot now belonging to a different circle of adherents, and she was but a mere *idikazi* (a loose woman with a child). There was no way an illustrious man like Gebashe would marry a damaged woman, a second-hand woman. Anyway, he was happily married already—or was he? Suddenly, Zama and their daughter, Sky, were some unbearable burden, an albatross around her neck.

The family council had arranged a date when the whole family would spend time with Gebashe. Lion, his family, and Naomi were also invited. Traditional beer was prepared for the occasion, and two sheep were slaughtered. It was a Saturday afternoon, and everyone was gathered in Speech's big lounge.

'Without divulging any secrets of the organization, we want you to tell us how you got involved in the struggle,' said Uncle Sam, addressing Gebashe.

'It's a long story, Uncle Sam, but I guess you have the whole Saturday afternoon to listen to it. Fezeka was still in NY 75 and not where it is now. Back then, it was a secondary school. A madman used to go past the school around lunch breaks. The learners would clap and chant, and he would dance and march down the street with the learners behind him. Their chant went like this:

'Leader: He-e-e, Sphithi! [Hey, Mr Riot!]
Chorus: Sphithi, kwenze njani? [Mr Riot, what's the matter?]
Leader: He-e-e, Sphithi!
Chorus: He-e-e, Sphithi, kwenze njani?
Leader: He-e-e, Sphithi!
Chorus: Sphithi, kwenze njani?
Leader: He-e-e, Sphithi!
Chorus: He-e-e, Sphithi, kwenze njani?
Dancer: Hu-u! Hu-u! Hu-u! Hu-u!

'This went on for several weeks until I got curious when the learners were gathered around this madman. I asked Mandla Moni what the learners were doing with the madman, and he invited me to come one evening and see for myself. Indeed, one Friday evening, I went with Mandla, and we visited a room at the men's hostel. What I heard there changed my life forever. We were actually attending a secret meeting of the revolution. We were addressed by a man who told us that our land had been taken by the whites and that we must fight to get it back. What surprised me most was that the madman was presiding over the meeting and was talking about us skipping the country and getting our education overseas in preparation for the new South Africa.

'It appeared that meetings had been held before, and arrangements to get some of the learners to cross the border had been made. Without asking if I agreed or not, Mandla introduced me to the members and stated that I was joining the recruits who were leaving in a week's time. A date was selected, and final arrangements were made. And that's how we left the country. I must say that I didn't understand much of what was stated as the reasons for our departure. I was just following others.

'Our first stop was Lesotho. But we left Lesotho after a couple of weeks and went to Zambia, then Tanzania, where we were taken to a school. When we finished high school, we went for training in the same country. That was where we again met Comrade Mazwi of the recruitment campaign at Fezeka, whom I had thought was a madman. Here everybody knew his chant, and we used it and others for training. That was also where Samson Ngaleka, one from our group, died from sunstroke.

'We were surprised when, as we were marching, he continued to march even after a command to halt. The instructor shouted at him, but he kept on marching, pleading, "Ndiyamatsha nje! Ndiyamatsha nje! Ndiyamatsha nje! [But I'm marching, sir!]" Our commanding officer was Comrade Sabelo Guma, and as soon as he saw that something was wrong, he was galvanized into action. By the time they got hold of Samson Ngaleka, the latter was quite disoriented. He died that evening in a hospital.

'This got me a little worried. I had not thought about death in exile till then, and the thought of dying away from my people horrified me. Thereafter, we were sent to different countries, where we pursued our various vocations. I went to Cuba to do medicine.

'When I finally got my degree, I wanted to be as close to home as possible. And that's how I got to Swaziland. After several years at a government hospital, I opened a private surgery. I've been working there until I came home. That is all you need to know about my life in exile. I'm now planning to settle permanently back home.'

'Then why did you not come back with everybody else?' asked Uncle Sam.

'I still need to discuss that with a few individuals important to my life first. Part of me actually wanted to come home, but the rest of me had experienced life in a free country and didn't want to lose that.'

People asked more questions, and Gebashe answered those that did not compromise the secret practices of the ANC. Naomi wanted to ask many questions, but she did not have the courage to find out if Gebashe would be free to marry her. Gebashe on his part was anxious that Naomi would refuse to marry him because he had been married to someone in Swaziland instead of waiting for her. He was hoping that though he was a divorcee, Naomi would still agree to marry him. But he could not summon enough courage to talk to Naomi and find out if she would marry him. His friends had told him that Naomi was likely to marry Zama soon. So he kept delaying meeting with her.

At the end of the family gathering, he found the opportunity to take Naomi aside. Once they were out of hearing of the other people, he said, 'Naomi! We haven't had a chance to talk ever since I returned home. Can I come to your flat tomorrow afternoon?'

'Yes, of course. You can come. At three o'clock I'll already have returned from church.'

'Okay, let it be three o'clock then.'

Indeed, at 3 p.m. on Sunday, Gebashe was knocking at Naomi's front door.

'I'm honoured to have you visit me despite your tight schedule,' said Naomi on opening the door.

'I'm the one that's honoured by your acceptance of my request to see you.'

'Can I get you a drink or coffee?'

'Coffee will be fine.'

When they were settled in the lounge, sipping coffee, Gebashe said, 'We were ordinary children of ordinary people when we were growing up, but the struggle transformed both our lives. I had to go into exile, and you had to stay and suffer with our people. And then what could have been a happy love life was destroyed even before we could realize it. Naomi, I love you. I want you to be my wife. I want us to start a new life together.'

'But, Gebashe, isn't it too late for us to do that? I have a child by another man who's promised to marry me, and I heard you have a wife in Swaziland too.'

'Yes, it's true that we are both in this situation, but it is not of our making. Call off the wedding with Zama. I have concluded divorce procedures with my wife. She didn't want to come to South Africa in the first place, which was a blessing to me, and she did not want me to come home, a sentiment that finally separated us. It's as if she knew instinctively that my rightful wife would be waiting for me here. Naomi, I do believe we were meant for each other. Can't we just start a new life with our new government and new dispensation and put all that's happened behind us? All is not lost, Naomi. There's always tomorrow.'

'Yes, I also want that, Gebashe. But it's going to be hard. Calling off a wedding with the father of my child is not going to be easy at all. And what happens to my child if I now get married to you?'

'Your child will be my child. She will come into the marriage, and she will enrich both our lives. I have two kids. They will come and go between us and their mother as much as they like. We didn't cause this to happen to us. Apartheid has ruined family lives. Look at Mandela, our icon. His family life is an absolute wreck. We too are having our own share of that.'

'But I'm an ordinary woman. I'm not a politician. Why should I be the one to experience this when I didn't choose to leave my family?'

'Apartheid has affected ordinary people like you and me. Its inheritance is visible in the whole nation, and even those who have been born to freedom are directly affected. What do you say about us, Naomi? I'm an ordinary person too. It wasn't my choice to be a soldier of the struggle.'

'Shouldn't we sort out ourselves first before we embark on this new road—pick up the pieces, so to speak?'

'If we accept each other into our lives, everything else will fall into place because we'll work on it together,' said Gebashe as he took Naomi into his arms and planted a permanent kiss on her lips. She responded by hugging and kissing him in return.

Suddenly, all the long years that had stood between them were melted by the hot embrace. For the first time, Naomi felt safe in the arms of the right man in her life. Many men and women to whom this was not to happen would have liked to feel the same as these two. At least for them, there was still a chance; there was still a tomorrow to look forward to.

CHAPTER 13

For Speech, there remained one thing to do—to take Gebashe home to his mother and father. This simple act of reconciliation would open the door for all the rites that have not been performed for his wife and kids to take place. So he approached Uncle Sam once again, and they invited the members of the family council to the latter's home. On the appointed day, all members of the family council were present. MaNdlovu prepared a special traditional meal for them. A sheep was slaughtered for the occasion.

The meeting was started with a prayer, and then Uncle Sam rose to address the meeting. He said the following words: 'My sisters, brothers, wives, and cousins, as you already know, there is nothing we can do in this house without you. You are the backbone of this family here in Cape Town. Speech and I are your life and blood. Our wives and children are your dependants. We therefore thank you for responding to our call and coming to hear what we have to say. We decided to call you so that you can help us determine if there is anything left to be done for the young man you see in our midst and who has been the reason for our joyful activities in the past few weeks. What is still left for us to do now is the question that is facing us at this meeting.' Then he sat down.

As soon as he sat down, Menzi, one of the senior men, stood up and said, 'You are speaking the truth, son of my father. We have done all we have done to welcome Gebashe home. But in truth, we haven't started to do the right thing. Gebashe's home is not Cape Town. To welcome him, we must go back to the roots, and that is KwaKhesa. The blessings of our elders await him there. I stop there.'

There was a long silence before Uncle Sam again stood up and said, 'You've hit the nail on the head, son of my father. What you are saying is what we also thought should be done now. As you know, Speech and I were expelled from home for having been the cause of Gebashe's disappearance. We were told never to set foot there without Gebashe. For years, we have lived under that spell. But now this son of the soil has been found. Therefore, we must take him home with us as he is our ticket to our home.'

Nomonde, one of the aunts in the larger family, was also at the meeting. She now rose to speak and said, 'We all agree that we should now take Gebashe home to his parents—our parents. We must present him to the graves of our ancestors. We must thank the ancestors appropriately for protecting him in foreign countries among strange people and races.'

'You will remember that when Gebashe left us, he was still a little boy and not yet ready to undertake initiation,' said Speech. 'He is now a fully grown family man, but he has still not been initiated. My cousin Uncle Sam and I were thinking therefore that we could deliver him to his parents when he comes back from initiation. But still, we must keep this a secret until the right moment.'

At this stage, Gebashe himself rose to his feet and said, 'My sisters, brothers, aunts, and cousins, I have already thanked you for the hero's welcome that I received, which in reality I don't think I deserve after deserting you and finding myself a better life in countries whose citizens were enjoying freedom. I have now grown up. I have a profession, a wife—that is, before I divorced her—and kids. But I have always known in my heart of hearts that without initiation, I will always be a little boy to you. I am looking forward to the custom that will give me my true identity, and I want to meet my parents as a man. But it's July now. I guess this will all happen in December? If that is true, then I must go back to Swaziland in the meantime and tie up a few loose ends in preparation for my permanent return home.'

A few more speakers added their voices to the resolution, and the meeting was closed. It had been decided that Speech would ask Khaya, who now worked in Johannesburg, to go home and ask Speech's father to allow him to perform at his house the initiation of a cousin who grew up in the city of Johannesburg. If the old man agreed, then preparations for a feast to welcome Gebashe from initiation would be made without his parents' awareness. The initiation of Ntsomi, Khaya's cousin, would be performed together with that of Gebashe. Everybody at the meeting believed that the old man would agree to Ntsomi's initiation as he had now mellowed down because of age and believed immensely in Khaya.

After the day of the meeting, Gebashe started preparing to open a surgery in Cape Town. He begged his ANC comrades to allow him to live a low-key life away from politics and parliament. This he was granted after much persuasion and pleading. He bought a building in Malunga Park, Gugulethu, and started renovations to make it a surgery.

He continued to live in Parow but started renovations to the house. Naomi helped him in every step to settle down.

While renovations were being done to his house and construction continued at his surgery, he went back to Swaziland to round up his business there. His discussion with Noni, his wife, was very painful indeed. But she agreed with him that they should go their separate ways and start new lives. She maintained that as she would not dream of going to SA, divorce had been the best option. They called the children and explained the whole situation to them. The surgery was sold, and they divided the proceeds between them. The children, Mbali and Sifiso, decided to spend some time with their mother before joining their father.

With Naomi, things were different. Zama heard from a friend that Naomi had an affair with someone she knew from childhood, a former freedom fighter. He heard how she was involved in welcoming this man back. He then decided on a date to come and pay the lobola (bride price) without consulting Naomi. He just called Lion and gave him the date. Thinking that he must have agreed with Naomi, Lion informed Zama that he would prepare for that day at his rural home in Baziya. Lion then called Naomi to ask her to help with the preparations.

'But, Bhuti, I know nothing about Zama's lobola! He can't organize something like that without me,' said Naomi, quite shocked by her brother's revelation.

'Didn't he speak to you first? I thought you had agreed with each other.'

'Not at all! Zama never came to me with the date. He made a marriage proposal, and I told him to wait.'

'Oh, my word! What are we going to do now?'

'I'll phone him and stop him. I was going to come to you and tell you that since Gebashe has returned, things have changed. I'm marrying Gebashe, Bhut' Lion.'

'Oh, is that so now? What about Sky?'

'Gebashe wants Sky to come with me, and I want his children to be part of the marriage.'

'Yeye, Bawo! [Oh, my father!] That's a nice little mess you've got yourself into. But will Zama allow you to just change your mind like that?'

'Blame it all on apartheid and the cursed spirit of freedom fighting. This isn't any of my making. Gebashe has divorced his wife. Anyway, she didn't want to come to SA in the first place.'

'Can you two build something positive out of the pieces from all these broken families? Anyway, come back to me after phoning Zama and let me know what you two have finally decided to do.'

Still furious at this news, Naomi called Zama immediately. 'What is this I hear that you have chosen a date to come and lobola me?' asked Naomi without making introductions.

'You seemed reluctant when I talked to you about a lobola. What was I supposed to do?'

'I wanted to sit down with you and discuss this in a civilized manner. But since you are so forward as to consult my family without my permission, I'll tell you over the phone. You and I being husband and wife is not on!'

'What do you mean not on? We spoke about this, and this has always been in our plans.'

'I've changed my mind. I'm not going to be your wife any more. Accept that.'

'Oh, do you have someone else? Do you have a hero that comes from never-never land? We stayed in this country. We suffered with our people and fought with them to free ourselves from bondage, and then there are those who ran away and now come back home as heroes.'

'So they've told you! The gossipmongers have told you!'

'Of course, I know about your welcoming parties and the excitement. But look here. We've got a child together, and you promised to marry me. I'll sue you for breach of promise if you dare stand in the way of my lobola.'

'You can't go ahead with this lobola. Didn't you hear that I don't want to marry you?'

'You wait and see! And if you refuse to marry me, I'll sue you!' Zama then called Lion to confirm the date when his people would be coming for the lobola.

When Lion called Naomi, she explained to him that she and Zama had not come to an agreement and that Zama was forcing matters. Lion was at a loss of what to do. In the end, he advised his sister to be at home in Baziya on the appointed day so that she could reject Zama more formally. Lion travelled together with Naomi in his car to Baziya.

On the appointed day, the men from Zama's clan arrived. They were driving a herd of ten live cattle. Zama had planned his lobola carefully. If he paid lobola in the form of money only, it could be easily rejected. But if his lobola was in the form of live cattle, it would be difficult to reject them. Besides, cattle are central in the tradition of lobola. They symbolize a bond with the ancestors of the two clans.

So Zama bought cattle from the farmers near Durban and trucked them to Mthatha. When *onozakuzaku* (the go-betweens) arrived at Naomi's home, they filled up the cattle kraal with a good breed of cattle. Then they were invited by the elders of Naomi's clan to the house to start the negotiations. When Lion informed the elders that Naomi was going to reject Zama, they were shocked.

'She cannot do that, Bhele [Lion's clan name]. Such a thing is never done. It brings misfortune to the clan. Besides, we'd be fools to reject so many cattle,' said Melikhaya, one of the elders.

When the negotiations started, the visitors declared that their son had seen a young woman in that house whom he would like to marry. The woman's name was Naomi.

'We are now going to ask our daughter if she knows your son,' said Vusumzi, one of the elders from Naomi's clan. Then they sent Lion to ask his sister if she wanted to get married to Zama.

Naomi responded by saying, 'Tell them I do not know this young man.'

'Are you sure about this, Sisi? Do you know that this means you will have to go into the cattle kraal and drive the cattle out?'

'I'm ready to do that if it means me retaining my freedom.'

Lion went back to the negotiating men and told his uncles what his sister had said.

'Our daughter says she does not know your son. So the negotiations will end here,' said Sithembiso to the visitors.

'Ha! Are you sure, Bhele, that we are talking about the same young woman? Surely our son cannot send us on such a long way if he is not sure!' said one of the men from the Khumalo clan.

'I am sure that we asked the right woman. Her name is Naomi, and she is a lawyer in Cape Town. Mtungwa [Khumalo clan name], our children do things differently these days. You never know what they are going to decide on. That is what freedom has brought us,' stated Melikhaya.

'Just give us a few minutes, people of the Bhele clan, to talk to our son on the phone. We'll go outside to do this,' said one of the visitors. They then filed out silently. When they came back, one of them said, 'People of the Bhele clan, we have spoken to our son, and we have agreed that if your daughter does not wish to marry our son, she knows what she must do. She must drive our cattle out of your cattle kraal.'

'Yes, we'll call her to come and do that. But before that happens, our women have prepared a meal for you. Wait for them to bring the meal so that we can eat,' said Mzobanzi, one of Naomi's uncles.

'Tell the young woman to take out our cattle from your cattle kraal. We are not here to eat food with you!' said one of the visitors bluntly.

So Naomi was instructed to take a stick and drive the cattle out of the cattle kraal. It was a sad sight for these families and for the neighbours, especially the men who loved the sight of cattle. The relatives and neighbours felt sorry for Naomi's mother in her state of health. She was plagued by short breath.

A few weeks after Naomi returned to Cape Town, a letter of demand was delivered to her. Zama was suing her for breach of promise. It was clear that Zama was prepared to make her suffer for rejecting him. Then followed the summons, and the date for the trial was 10 December. That made things worse because Gebashe would not be there to give her moral support. By that date, he would be at the initiation school. Naomi suffered much stress because of this.

CHAPTER 14

In November, Gebashe returned to Cape Town with his children, Mbali and Sifiso. Preparations had been finished for his initiation. His father had agreed when Khaya asked for permission to initiate his cousin. Ntsomi arrived in due course at Meshack's home and was accompanied by Khaya and the other young men of the family to the bush.

With the Hlubi and Sotho of Matatiele and Mount Fletcher, boys are initiated in large groups which gather at the home of a chosen initiate. The chosen homestead becomes the host for the initiation. When the boys return from initiation, they will visit each other's homes as one group, and they will sing and do praise poetry. These visits are accompanied by much feasting and celebration. If a boy arrives from a boarding school or work after the other boys have already gone to the bush, he can join them without having to come home first.

So Gebashe would arrive after the other boys had gone to the bush and join them there. This meant that he did not have to come home until the initiation was over.

On 24 November, the boys were prepared for the bush school, and at dawn the following day, they were ushered into their bush hut. They were using the home of Mthetho, a member of the Khesa clan, as their base and host residence. On 24 November, Gebashe, together with a column of men, started the journey from Cape Town to KwaKhesa. They travelled by a hired combi, a group of nine men, plus the driver, Speech. Uncle Sam was also among the men.

When they arrived in the town of Matatiele on 25 November, they waited until late in the afternoon before starting the last leg of their journey. They had planned to park the combi at a village called Sidakeni, which was before KwaKhesa, and then proceed to the bush school in the mountains on foot. When they approached the school, they sang a mountain song as is the custom, and the initiates started singing in response. As soon as they got into the hut, Gebashe had to take off his tracksuit and was given a blanket and a cow's skin to cover himself before joining the other initiates. Khaya was also at the initiation school, and he was for the umpteenth time cautioned not to mention Gebashe's presence at home. The instructors at the bush school had also been forewarned against telling at home about Gebashe's presence at the bush school.

There was going to be a big feast to welcome the initiates back home after several weeks in the bush. Khubelo and the other girls were now all married. Khubelo had come home to help Khaya prepare for the ceremony. She was, however, not told anything about Gebashe for fear that the news of his presence might spread. Sarah and Meshack were now too old to help with anything. Khaya was now their only son, and he looked after them. He lived with his wife, Nophumzile, in Johannesburg and came home only during the Christmas season to take care of any matters that needed attention. Nophumzile too had come home to prepare for the ceremony, but she too thought that it was only for Ntsomi.

'I hope your cousin will choose to live with us after the initiation. We had two sons in addition to you, but they were both swallowed up by the world. If you were not here, grandson, we would have no one to look after us,' said the old man one day as they were discussing the preparations for the returning ceremony.

'You are like mother and father to me. That is why I care for you so much. You brought me up from a four-year-old boy, and now I am a fully grown man. I'll never leave you whatever happens,' replied Khaya.

'If Speech and Gebashe were still with us, they would be helping you now with this ceremony. How I wish my sons were not so rebellious. Now I will go to my grave without seeing my own child, Speech. As for Gebashe, he died young like his elder sister. We never even had a chance to bury his bones. He just vanished from the face of the earth.'

'Please don't talk like that. Gebashe is still alive . . . I mean, it could happen, Grandpa, that Gebashe didn't die. Perhaps you will see him one day before you go to your grave.'

'There's not a chance. If he was still alive, he would have come home by now.'

'At least Bhut' Speech is right here . . . in Cape Town. You can always invite him to come home.'

'If Speech cared about us, he would have come home to see us. My son is full of arrogance and self-importance. He knows very well that we shall soon depart from this world and that we would like to see him before that happened. The children God has given me are so self-centred.'

'I'm sure Bhut' Speech wants to come and see you. It's not easy for one to bring up children without the blessing of one's parents. I'm sure he would like to come home and see you. He must miss you very much. Only his sense of guilt about what he did to you keeps him from coming home.'

Thus would the conversation go between Khaya and his grandfather. Khaya mentioned to the old man that the initiates would visit the old man's home. According to custom, when initiates visit a homestead, they come in the middle of the night because they must not be seen by the women and children. They stand by the cattle kraal and start intoning mountain songs. They have to hum the songs so that nobody can recognize the voices of individuals.

Indeed, one night the initiates came to Meshack's home. They had come to ask for a sheep for meat to eat at the bush school. Meshack and a few men who were with him approached the initiates near the cattle kraal but because of the darkness, he could not see each initiate. He spoke to them and greeted them as a group, and they responded by singing more mountain songs.

When Gebashe found himself so close to his father and yet so distant from him because of the prescriptions of the custom, his eyes were filled with tears. He heard his father greeting them, and yet he could not greet back or run to him to hug him. On his part, Meshack did not know that he was in the presence of both his sons, as Speech was there too. The latter felt like running to his father and hugging him, but it had been agreed that he would remain anonymous throughout this visit. He felt a pang of nostalgia as his feet once again stood on the ground he used to stand on as a little boy. He too felt the tears in his eyes and was grateful for the darkness which hid his face from everybody. The women, keeping their distance, stood in front of the huts and ululated. They were not allowed to go near the initiates.

At the end of the visit, the initiates and the young men who accompanied them sang a marching song and marched into the dark night. Early in the morning the following day, Meshack ordered Khaya to send a sheep to the mountain school for meat.

Preparations for the initiates' return home were made. Khaya was busy organizing the ox to be slaughtered on the day of their return. The women brewed traditional beer and baked bread for the occasion. First, the initiates would be welcomed at the home of the host for the night. The following day, they would dress up in their new clothes as *amakrwala* (newly initiated young men), and then they would be smeared with ochre.

When smeared with ochre, it is not easy to identify *ikrwala*, and since Gebashe left home as a little boy, the men were confident that the women would not recognize him. The newly initiated young men would then start singing and reciting their praise poems. Gebashe had been instructed to do only standard praise poems at the home of the host, but at his own home, he would do the special praise poem that he had been specially practising at the mountain school. Speech was not to join the initiates until they came to his home.

At last, the great day came. The women were ululating, and the men were singing. The men brought a chair for Meshack, the old man, to sit on. The performance of the initiates took place on the open grounds between the huts and the cattle kraal. The initiates started singing and reciting their praise songs. When it was Ntsomi's turn, the crowd stood on its feet. Everybody knew that this was the climax of the performance and that Ntsomi would be the last *ikrwala* to perform because it was at his home. After doing his performance to the delight and satisfaction of everybody, Ntsomi went back to take his place among the newly initiated.

Now everybody was talking at the same time, and the women were making remarks about how Ntsomi looked so much like his father. Some of them had started moving back to their pots, thinking that the performance was over. At that moment, Gebashe stepped to the front of the newly initiated and the crowd, and he lifted his club to begin his performance. Then a strange thing happened. Speech emerged from the cattle kraal. As soon as the crowd recognized him, they fell silent. Those who had started to move away came running back.

Speech was covered with a new blanket and a man's hat on his head. He carried a club in his right hand and a spear with another club in his left hand. This was quite unexpected, and people gasped with shock as it was generally known that Speech had been rejected by his old man and had stayed in Cape Town for close to ten years.

As soon as he appeared, Speech made straight for the old man, stood in front of him, and said, 'My father, I greet you in the name of our ancestor, Nozulu. I am your son Speech. I have returned! Your son and heir has come home. I bring with me my wife and kids. But more than that, I bring with me your long-lost son, without whom you ordered me never to return to your house. Gebashe, you are back home after many years in exile. Do your thing now, my brother!'

People gasped with shock and excitement. The women started ululating and saying the praises of the Khesa clan. Meshack rose to his feet, speechless as he stared at Speech and looked at the newly initiated young man in front of him.

After a long pause, he exclaimed, 'Ye, Madoda! Ngumntwan' am uSpeech lo? Ingaba ngenene nguy' umntwan' am lo?' My good fellows! Is this my child, Speech? Could this indeed be my child? Where is this Gebashe you are talking about, my child?

At that moment, Gebashe took a few more steps forward so that he stood only about three metres from his father and, with his club raised in front of him, he started singing.

Gebashe: Awo-o! Awo-o! Aphelil' amathemba!
Chorus: Ye-e! Buya-a! Ye-e! Buya-a!
Gebashe: Awo-o! Awo-o! Aphelil' amathemba!
Chorus: Ye-e! Buya-a! Ye-e! Buya-a!
Gebashe: Baxelele bangezi. Bathath' inkomo zodwa.
Chorus: Ye-e! Buya-a! Ye-e! Buya!

> Tsir-r-r-r! Tsipha-a-a!
> So says Gebashe, the vagabond.
> Gebashe is his name; Gebashe is his clan.
> I'm the one that defied the instructions of
>   his father.
> I'm the one that disobeyed his father
> and went to school in strange lands.
> Among strange tribes of Africa, I thrived
> like the pigweed growing among untamed
>   weeds.
> I am the cub of a lion of Africa,

and as a young lion, I roar.
When I left, my father was a young man.
Now I'm back; I'm the young man, and
    he's an elder.
I am the deserter who abandoned my people
in time of suffering,
hoping to acquire skills for reconstruction.
My mother is a quiet woman.
She could have stopped me, but she did not.
In my veins runs the blood of an African.
I have earned that identity through hardship.
Speech, I love you, for you opened doors
    for me.
Speech, I respect you, for you lent a hand
    to the struggle.
Speech, I admire you, for you risked the old
    man's wrath.
Speech, I'm indebted to you, for you
    brought me back
to my fatherland.
Tsir-r-r-r! Tsipha-a-a!

As a rule, an African does not show his emotion. But for Meshack, this was unimaginable. He sank back on his chair, his hands cupping his head, and he cried like a child. Speech wanted to go forward and hug his father in the manner comrades did, but he was checked by the knowledge that the old man was a conservative man and would not understand. That he was crying was sufficient demonstration of affection. True Africans do not hug—that is the white people's expression of emotions. An irresistible urge made Speech come forward and take the old man's hand.

From the moment Gebashe ended his praise-singing, there was an outburst of ululations from the crowd, and people sang the praises of the Khesas and those of his mother, the Mthimkhulus. Everybody was excited and full of praise. When Speech knelt down to hold his father's hand, there was a fresh burst of ululation and praise-singing from the crowd. Gebashe, as an initiate, was not allowed to greet people with his hand. It was sufficient for them to listen to his praise-singing and to ululate from a distance. This was the custom.

Gebashe was the last *ikrwala* to do the praise-singing. His mother, Sarah, was also overcome by tears. Her daughters tried to comfort her, but they too could not hold back their tears of joy. This affected many people, and they broke down crying.

After Gebashe's praise-singing, an opportunity was given to Meshack to address the initiates. Normally, after the last initiate has done his praise-singing, the festivities would begin in earnest. But this occasion was special. It marked the reunion of father and sons. So Meshack rose from his seat, took a few steps, and stood in front of the initiates, who were now seated.

Then he said, 'My children, before I speak, I would like you, Speech, to come and sit here with the initiates. Speech, come and sit here next to Gebashe. My joy today—and I'm sure your mother's joy today—is like the joy we had when you two were born. We had given up and thought we would never see you again until we died. To us, this is a miracle.

It is the greatest reward our free country has given us—to bring both our sons back to us.

'Now we are ready to die, knowing full well that Speech and Gebashe will bury us and look after the rest of the family. We know that we are lucky parents to have both of you come back to us alive. Some parents have to bury the bones of their children while others don't even have any bones to bury. We have lived with anxiety all our lives in not knowing what was happening to our children and relatives in the towns and cities of this country. But now all is forgiven. Your mother and I will go to our graves with happy hearts, knowing that we are leaving our land in the good hands of our children.

'I am addressing you all, my children, when I say that you are a generation of reconstruction. In my sorrow, I chased away my son Speech, not knowing that what I did in anger would haunt me throughout my life. All I can say to you, Speech, is that you must know that behind the iron curtain, there is a tender heart. Welcome home, my son. I had even forgotten that I had said you shouldn't come home without Gebashe. All I wanted now was to bring you back to my house, your home, before I died. Now Gebashe is the greatest gift that you have given us, your parents. No child can ever do what you have done for his parents. For that, we can only say thank you. May your endeavours be blessed.'

At this point, the old man broke down again and cried. Other seniors helped him back to his chair.

When Gebashe returned to Cape Town, he had to give moral support to Naomi, who was going through a difficult time with a court case, where she was charged for breach of promise. At some stage, Gebashe, Speech, and Lion had a meeting with Zama in an attempt to settle the matter out of court. But Zama was adamant, and they had to give up.

The case took many months before it came to court. In the meantime, Gebashe and Naomi prepared for the wedding. When they spoke to Sky to find out if she would be happy with the wedding, she agreed. So the marriage was now a certainty, and no one could stop it. Meshack selected two elders from the Khesa clan to go and negotiate with Naomi's people, and a herd of ten cattle as lobola were paid. This time Naomi accepted the bridegroom, and the negotiations proceeded without any hindrance.

Gebashe and Naomi were also planning to relocate to Matatiele. Gebashe wanted to start a surgery at KwaKhesa, and Naomi was going to join a firm of attorneys in town. Arrangements with Nakin and Associates were already underway. Their aim was to develop the rural villages in Matatiele and to promote farming. Speech was also planning to return to his home to develop it while he and his wife continued to work in Cape Town.

The trial was a bitter experience for Naomi. Zama was determined to give her a hard time. What helped her was a case that the University of Cape Town opened against Zama for plagiarism while he had been a student there. So Zama was now faced with two court cases and was battling to convince the magistrates in both of them.

Mr Solwa, Naomi's attorney, in making the concluding argument, stated the following: 'Your Worship, there is no doubt in my mind that Miss Noyanda and Dr Nyaluza were meant for each other. Both of them were the victims of apartheid, and their destinies were shaped for them by the politicians and the freedom fighters of their time. Miss

Noyanda had no control over what happened to her, Your Worship. She struck a relationship with Mr Khumalo, believing that she would never see Dr Nyaluza again. But when Dr Nyaluza turned up while she was still single, she saw an opportunity for her to fulfil her life's desire and marry the man of her dreams. Many people's family lives have been destabilized by apartheid as some of them went to prison, some into exile, and others to the urban areas to look for work. Our legendary leader, Mandela, is a leading example of this. Twice he has experienced broken marriages, and they were not of his making. Similarly, Miss Noyanda here experienced a complex situation because the man of her dreams had to go into exile.'

When it was the turn of Zama's lawyer to make a concluding argument, he shocked everyone when he said, 'My client has a request to make, Your Worship. My client has reconsidered his complaint and concurs that Miss Noyanda may not have been meant for him. He therefore wishes to withdraw the case and to negotiate out of court for the child.'

After many questions, the magistrate accepted Zama's request. In that way, the case was settled out of court. When Sky's parents asked her whom she wanted to live with, she chose her mother. That meant that Zama could visit as a family friend, and Sky could visit him at will. Admittedly, this was a complex marriage, but how better could Naomi and Gebashe have done to make their lives happier? Now Gebashe and Naomi could concentrate on the preparations for the wedding. There was still time for them to enjoy what remained of their lives together.

It was Naomi and Gebashe's wedding day at Naomi's home in Mthatha. The relatives were there, young and old; friends, colleagues, and comrades in the struggle were there. In the evening, everybody attended the reception at the Mandela Museum Hall at Qunu. There was a long programme with family speakers, friends, and government people. Mandla was the programme director.

After the main meal, when desserts were served, Mandla came to the microphone and said, 'We are now going to propose a toast, and this is the last item on the programme. It is also the moment I have been waiting for all evening. Soon enough, you will know the reason why. We Xhosa people are lovers of folktales. I am now going to ask Comrade Sabelo Guma to propose a toast. While we were in parliament in Cape Town, I asked Comrade Guma to come to the wedding of Comrade Naomi and Comrade Gebashe specifically to propose a toast, and he agreed. And now let us put our hands together for Comrade Guma.'

There was applause as Guma came to the microphone while everybody started filling their glasses with champagne.

After the usual introduction, Guma said, 'I'm going to propose a toast, but let me first tell you a story as our programme director has suggested. I was a young man of twenty-five. Having trained in Russia for six years, I was then posted on a mission to Cape Town, my place of birth. It was a Sunday afternoon, and I had just buried a cache of weapons in the bush near Langa. I was working alone as this was a sensitive part of the mission. I was busy marking the location when I heard a girl scream not far from where I was. I took Father Freedom [the AK-47] with me and approached cautiously. Right in front of me at a clearing in the bush,

I saw about six or seven tsotsis brutally assaulting a young boy who, at a guess, must have been about seventeen and a young girl of about fifteen. I waited behind the bush, not knowing what exactly to do. I didn't want anybody in the township to know my whereabouts, and yet these children desperately needed my help. I waited anxiously to see if anybody would be coming. It was a Sunday afternoon, and the bush was a no-go area for township residents. From where I was, both the boy and the girl seemed to have been beaten and stabbed unconscious, and these savages set about raping the unconscious girl. It was this sordid act that forced me to reveal myself.

'With hands in the air, I cried, "Hayini, majita! Senibajinda, maan, brothers! Basebancinci aba bantwana." [Please, gentlemen, leave them alone, brothers! These children are still too young.]

'"Ungubani wena, mgodoyi! [Who are you, you mongrel!] You think you can just come and tell us what to do? We'll show you," said the leader, quickly adjusting his trousers and coming for me, his knife in the air. I quickly collected Father Freedom from my feet, and as soon as the rascals saw what I had in my hands, they scattered and disappeared into the bush. I could have mowed them down easily with my weapon, but I didn't want to be discovered. Instead I aimed a few shots in the air.

'Skollies are cowards. When they find themselves in danger, all they can think of is running for their lives. And all they can do is victimize helpless people. After hiding my gun, I ran to the bus terminus to make a call to my colleague, and he brought transport. We cleaned up everything, and we took the two children, who were both still in a coma, to

Groote Schuur Hospital. We were sure they were both going to die from their injuries. We gave false addresses and left to finish our own mission. Mandla was the first person other than those who were at the mission with me, all dead now, to hear the story, and when I told it to him at a ceremony on Robben Island last month, he said he would like me to repeat the same story at Comrade Gebashe's wedding.'

Here Mandla broke in and said, 'When you told me this story, Comrade Guma, I did not want to tell you what I had heard when I was still a schoolboy in Cape Town. All I wish to do just now is to ask Comrade Naomi and Comrade Gebashe if this folktale is true. And that was the reason why I asked Comrade Guma to tell this story while proposing a toast.'

You could have heard a pin fall. Then a voice rang out, crying, 'Speech!' Another one followed it and another and yet another until the whole audience was crying out for a speech by Naomi and Gebashe. But when Gebashe rose to speak, one would not imagine this to be the same audience when it now fell silent as a grave.

'All I can say, Comrade Mandla,' said Gebashe, his whole face exuding confidence in its entirety, 'is that the jigsaw puzzle is now complete, and the wounds are sure to heal, aren't they, Naomi darling? There's always tomorrow—whatever happens.'